TERROR MOUNTAIN

A NOVEL BY

FRED L. FUNK

TATTERSALL PUBLISHING
Denton, Texas

For information, contact:
Tattersall Publishing
225 W. Hickory St., Ste. 131
Denton, Texas 76201
www.tattersallpub.com

This book is a work of fiction. Names, characters, places and incidents are either products of the author's imagination or are used fictitiously. Any resemblance to actual events or locales, or persons living or dead, is entirely coincidental.

Cover and interior design by Crystal Wood

ISBN 978-1-7320129-2-9

DEDICATION

This book is dedicated to my late uncle by marriage, Dale Green. Dale spent many years in law enforcement and told me many interesting tales. Many of those stories are incorporated in *Terror Mountain*. This work is also dedicated to Dale's beautiful wife Judy, who lived the nightmare as a member of the jury in the case that inspired this novel. Dale and Judy, this one is for you.

BOOKS BY FRED L. FUNK

MINISTRY AND MOONSHINE

MOONSHINERS' REVENGE

MOONSHINE MEMORIES

LIFE AND DEATH ON CANNON CREEK

THE THROWAWAY SON

JUSTICE FOR CASSIE

EPHRIM'S JOURNEY

TERROR MOUNTAIN

LETTIE'S SIN *(Late 2018)*

CHAPTER 1

THE BIRTH OF A LEGEND

RICHARD HERRON'S DARK, PENSIVE EYES REMAINED WIDE OPEN with an evil stare, but his body went limp. The prison doctor pronounced the inmate dead at 12:01AM, Thursday, April 22, 2009. Three decades had passed since the time he committed unthinkable crimes. Even though the wheels of the Colorado judicial system had turned slowly, Gil Gentry knew that justice for Marcia Leggett had at long last been served. The retired sheriff of Lake County took no real pleasure in the execution; the victim still lay dead in the Evergreen Cemetery on the northwestern edge of Leadville, and thirty years later her family still mourned.

Justice was a long time coming and I'm glad it's finally over, Gil thought as memories of the unforgettable night Herron committed the horrific rape and murder flooded his mind. Everything related to the crime that had transpired since played like a bad movie in his head. Thirty years later vivid visions of the victim's mutilated body still haunted the former sheriff and it seemed to him that it had only happened yesterday.

In all his years as a lawman Gil had never investigated an act so heinous. Over his years as sheriff he had become legendary for the hundreds of villains he tracked down and arrested. In all that time, he had never apprehended a perpetrator as evil as Richard Herron. The case affected Gil so negatively that at one point in his career he questioned his continued work in the field of law enforcement. At times, the dedicated lawman wanted to shoot or hurt in some

1

way the scum that he arrested instead of leaving the punishment to the judicial system. His personal brand of justice seemed especially appropriate for the perps who committed crimes against children and those ungodly acts that involved rape or murder. It seemed to Gil that too often punishments meted out to the criminals did not measure up to the severity of the offenses.

What made a man born and raised in the peaceful rolling countryside of North Central Texas become a sheriff in the Rocky Mountain town of Leadville, the county seat of Lake County Colorado? What events in his life brought him to its current point? *Something in my upbringing is bound to have something to do with it,* Gil thought as stories that he had been told about his birth and childhood flooded his memory.

* * *

Eight-year-old Virginia Hilton wondered why her mother, who normally dressed fashionably in current styles, had adopted large, blousy attire. "What are you staring at?" the mother snapped as the daughter observed the woman's expanded midsection.

"Just wondering why you're getting so big around the middle and why you're wearing those big ol' dresses."

"Shut your mouth, girl. Don't be vulgar."

The daughter grew silent and confused. What had she said that her mother considered vulgar, and why would she not explain? It seemed to the girl that the change in the woman's clothing occurred not too long after a young man, Allen Gentry, joined the family as her stepfather.

Rose's marriage to Hank Hilton lasted only long enough that it produced two offspring, Virginia and her younger sister Maggie. Hank departed his earthly existence as Virginia reached the age of four and Maggie had not had her first birthday. Ginnie, as she was known by family and friends, did not share her mother's happiness with Allen, since the day her father died three years earlier still haunted her young mind.

"Ginnie, give your father a cup of water. He's not feeling well," Rose had instructed.

"Yes, ma'am," the daughter answered dutifully as she filled a metal dipper with water from a bucket that sat on a Hoosier cabinet that stood against one wall of the kitchen. After Ginnie poured the liquid into a cup, she carried it to her father, who sat in a chair with his head resting on a small round wooden table in the center of the room. "Here, Daddy. Here's you a drink of water," she offered as she placed the container in front of the man, but he did not respond.

"Did you get your father a drink?" the mother asked from an adjoining room.

"Yes, Mother," the daughter answered. "But, he isn't drinking it and he's not saying a word. He looks like he's asleep."

"What do you mean?" Rose asked as she entered the kitchen.

"He's just sitting there with his head on the table sound asleep," Ginnie replied.

As soon as Rose observed her husband and felt his cold gray face she realized that her beloved had departed this world for a better life in another realm. At her tender age Ginnie remembered little else about that day except some men in dark suits carried her father from the house. Her mother and grandparents, Momma and Papa Wentworth, only told the child that her father had gone to be with Jesus. They offered no further explanation

Allen Gentry had harbored a secret crush on Rose Wentworth since their school days. Rose had paid little attention to the boy two years younger and he had not professed his feelings for fear of rejection or ridicule. His heart broke when the girl of his dreams married Hank Hilton, an older man with a grown daughter and a son still in high school. When a period of time considered decent had passed after Hank died, leaving Rose with two young children, the suitor decided that the age difference no longer mattered so he courted the object of his affection. The brief courtship resulted in the accidental conception of the future legendary lawman, Gil Gentry, and a hasty marriage followed.

Allen Gentry, a young, rather gruff, and headstrong husband, felt that he needed some distance between himself and Rose's parents. In view of the circumstances that prompted their daughter's marriage, they looked on him scornfully. He sought a degree of independence that he did not feel while he lived in the same household as his in-laws. Fortunately for the son-in-law, his mechanical skills secured him a job at an automobile dealership in San Angelo, Texas.

Ginnie's sensitive young ears heard the contentious conversation that spoiled the pleasant evening enjoyed by the family. They spent most hours after supper and before bedtime on the large front porch of their home and enjoyed the cool April breezes. The young girl realized that her stepfather's announcement did not please her grandparents.

"I've got myself a job doing mechanic work at the Ford dealer in San Angelo," Allen announced.

"How long will you be gone?" His father-in-law asked.

"For as long as they are happy with me and my work, I reckon," the son-in-law answered.

"Do you think it's a good idea for you to go off and leave Rose and the kids? After all, y'all have just married and she is expecting."

"I'm not going to leave them. They're coming with me."

"You didn't think you should talk this over with us before you made a decision?" Wentworth questioned.

"The decision was mine to make and nobody else's," Allen

snapped. "I've already arranged for a place to live. They've renovated and turned the officers' quarters at old Fort Concho into family housing and I've rented one of the units." The family sat in stunned silence as Allen continued. "The job starts the first week of May so we'll be taking the train at the end of the month."

"What's mother expecting?" Ginnie asked innocently.

Momma Wentworth spoke. "When two people love each other and marry. . . ."

Papa Wentworth shot his wife a stare and interrupted. "Be quiet, child. We don't talk about such things."

"We don't talk about what things?" Ginnie questioned persistently.

"Things a little girl doesn't need to know about. Now be quiet."

Allen knew that he had upset Rose's father when the quiet, soft-spoken man simply arose from his chair, turned and walked into the house without uttering another word. His mother-in-law, on the other hand, spoke up in a deliberate but civil manner.

"Allen, what are you thinking? After what you've already done to Rose and this family, and now you're taking her away? She is due the first part of June and she needs to be here with us."

"What did Allen do? What do you mean she's due?" The granddaughter asked insistently.

"I told you before, don't be vulgar," Rose barked.

"Papa told you, Ginnie. We don't talk about such things," Momma Wentworth reminded halfheartedly. "Now be quiet." Had it not been for the grandfather's admonition, the more outspoken grandmother probably would have explained the pregnancy to the child.

"I'm sorry, but it is a damn good job with good pay and the decision has been made. We will be leaving," Allen informed bluntly.

"Watch your tongue, Allen. There are big ears listening."

Ginnie realized that her grandmother had referred to her ears, but she did not think that they were big.

"What about you, Rose? What do think about it?" Momma questioned.

"Momma, I have to go where my husband goes," the daughter answered. "I sure hope you and Papa understand."

"You will regret it," the mother replied sharply as she remembered how unhappy she had been when her father moved the family from Tennessee to Texas. She left a boyfriend and a life she dearly loved behind. She had no idea of the level of regret that would be felt by Allen and the entire family months later.

Ginnie hated leaving her beloved grandparents, but excitement filled her being as she knew with the move new adventures lay ahead. *I wonder what Mama is expecting and what's due in June and why can't we talk about it,* she thought as she drifted off to sleep while visions of life in a fort engulfed her young mind. She wondered if there would be soldiers and Indians since she had learned about them in school. *Sure hope the Indians are friendly.*

A single tear trickled down Papa Wentworth's cheek while he stood silent and stoic on the platform at the Denison, Texas train depot as he and Momma bid their daughter and granddaughters goodbye. Had he realized the outcome of the move the quiet man would have been more verbal with his objections. Ginnie held Maggie's hand as they boarded the train that took them on the road to what she considered exciting new adventures.

As the train rounded a curve, Ginnie watched in electrified wonderment as large puffs of smoke ascended from the coal-fired engine that powered the conveyance. It formed a long trail of gray and black vapors as the locomotive chugged along the tracks. She looked intently from the window of the train at the rolling countryside filled with alternating areas of large timber and lush pastures where herds of cattle grazed on the sweet green grasses. The confused but excited girl knew that the only home she had ever known lay behind her when the rails brought the family to Sherman.

The Missouri-Kansas-Texas Railroad train, known as the Katy, proceeded south from the North Texas area near the Red River towards Dallas. The young girl observed more houses, large buildings, cars, and flurries of people than she had ever seen as the train moved through the city and arrived at Dallas Union Station. The cloud of gray smoke from the locomotive and the heavy stench of burning coal that permeated the atmosphere choked the girls as they stepped off the train. Ginnie observed her mother with deep concern when she had a coughing fit as the polluted air swirled about and filled her lungs.

"You girls stay close," Allen instructed as the family got off the Katy and headed to another platform where they boarded the Atchison, Topeka and the Santa Fe train that carried the travelers westward through Cowtown, the city of Ft. Worth.

As the train left the large cities behind, Ginnie viewed a landscape much different than the area around Denison where she had always lived. Her former home had been surrounded by large timber of oak, pecan, and hickory, but she now observed a countryside dotted by mesquite and almost devoid of larger trees. Buffalo grass that grew close to the ground paled in comparison to the lush fields of coastal Bermuda that encompassed the area around her home town. Visions of her grandparent's hillside house that had a terraced lawn filled with iris, japonica, forsythia, crepe myrtle, and many other flowers flooded her mind. Each species bloomed in season, but those images faded as her life-long home became a distant memory.

Thoughts of frequent visits to Woodlake, a small reservoir and recreational area near where she lived, engulfed Ginnie's mind as she starred at the dry lands that seemed like a totally different world to the wide-eyed youngster. She daydreamed of Indians with painted faces who shouted war whoops as they attacked the train and soldiers who rode to the rescue on horseback, shot at the savages, and chased them away.

Dust from the dry red earth that enveloped the area swirled around their feet as the family disembarked from the train. Ginnie felt a degree of disappointment since no soldiers greeted them when they arrived at Fort Concho, and no hostile Indians surrounded them.

"Where are the soldiers?" she asked as they arrived at the old fort. "When will the Indians attack?"

"There are no soldiers," the mother answered. "And what makes you think Indians are going to attack?"

"We read about 'em in school, but I guess the Indians around here must be friendly."

"Ginnie, there are no Indians and no soldiers. I just don't know where you get these ideas."

A large porch spanned the front of the renovated officer's quarters and the shade of a large mesquite tree in front of the sandstone structure offered a good place as a playground for Ginnie and her younger sister. The low-lying, sprawling branches looked perfect for climbing to the girl. Even though the West Texas sun brought extreme heat to the air and dry arid earth, thick stone walls kept the interior of the home relatively cool. It appeared as a suitable dwelling, but Ginnie wanted soldiers and Indians.

She did not ask about the situation, since she remembered her grandfather's rebuke, but in Ginnie's eyes it appeared that her mother had become extremely large around her middle. It appeared to the girl that Rose's belly kind of pooched out in front, and the clothes she wore appeared almost as tents. The daughter desperately desired exploration of the fort and its old buildings, but her mother seemed exhausted and ill most of the time, so the dutiful girl remained close and helped with household chores. As weeks passed, the expectant mother turned over most house cleaning and meal preparation to the now-nine-year-old. The girl also shouldered the role as caregiver to her little sister who, at her young age, had no responsibilities. Ginnie's new adventures had turned from fun-filled and exciting days to a time of work and drudgery.

To young Ginnie, the blazing sun seemed much hotter than it did in North Texas and sleep came with great difficulty. Many nights the heat kept her awake and sweat soaked her nightgown and the sheets on her bed. As she desperately sought rest, thoughts ran amuck in her innocent young mind. *Sure miss Momma and Papa, and what I wouldn't give for a day at Woodlake, swimming, picnicking, and riding the carousel. There was supposed to be Indians and soldiers out here in this hot country. At least they woulda caused some excitement. Something is terribly wrong with Mama. She's got bigger and bigger around her middle, she looks like she's gonna pop, she's tired all the time, and I have to do her chores. What's gonna happen when she's "due." Why won't somebody tell me what's going on?*

Ginnie finally fell asleep, only to be awakened by the sound of a strange voice in the house. Low moans and groans along with an occasional hair-raising scream by her mother wafted through the air, followed by a baby's cry. She never really understood why, but suddenly it all became crystal clear to the young girl. The strange voice belonged to a doctor who assisted with the birth as Gilbert Allen Gentry made his appearance on June 7, 1929. Ginnie instinctively knew that she and Maggie now had a baby brother and she was not pleased. The girl had already been saddled with the responsibility as caregiver for her younger sister, and she correctly surmised that care of her infant brother had been added to the many chores she performed.

Rose Lee Wentworth Hilton Gentry had been pampered her entire life. Her parents had provided her every need and desire and they had assumed much of the parental role with Ginnie and Maggie. Hank Hilton, Rose's first husband whose age was exceeded by that of Momma Wentworth by only three months, also doted over her. Allen Gentry, who had a brash personality, did not often bend to the wishes of others, not even those of his wife. Rose looked to her older daughter for relief from many of her responsibilities as wife and mother.

"Ginnie, come in here," Rose's voice came from inside the house as Ginnie sat in a rope swing that hung from a limb of the large mesquite tree in the front yard.

"What do you need?" Ginnie asked.

"Your brother needs changing. His diaper is full."

"But, Mama, why can't you change it? It makes me want to throw up every time."

"Mama doesn't feel well," Rose answered pitifully. "Come on in here and take care of your brother. It's about all I can do to feed him, just drains my strength every time."

"Why does it make you feel weak just because he eats?" The daughter asked innocently.

"Shut your mouth, girl. I just do not understand why you are so vulgar."

"But, Mama, I just . . ."

"Shut up," Rose demanded. "And while you're at it, your brother needs a bath."

The obedient daughter jumped from the swing and reluctantly entered the house and completed the distasteful tasks. She removed the soiled diaper, placed little Gil in a wash basin, bathed, and diapered him. As she placed her brother back in his cradle he screamed.

"Ginnie, will you please do something with him? My head hurts, and that squalling doesn't help." The dutiful daughter removed the baby from the crib, took him and a blanket to the front porch where she made a pallet for the infant.

As summer relinquished its time and fall descended on San Angelo, Ginnie pushed ideas of childhood play to the deep recesses of her mind and assumed the role fate had handed her. Cooking, cleaning, washing diapers, and caring for Maggie and Gil dominated her life and left little time for normal childhood pursuits. She had slowly developed a love for the baby brother who had invaded her world, but more like a caregiver's love than a sister's. Although she cared deeply for the boy, she harbored some resentment at the responsibilities heaped upon her by her mother.

The highly intelligent Ginnie looked forward to the start of a new school year and she considered that time spent in the classroom rescued her, at least temporarily, from the tasks at home. As a first grader in Denison she scored several grades higher on tests and the school administration double promoted her to the third grade. As the beginning of school drew closer, Ginnie's excitement accelerated until Rose put a damper on it.

"Ginnie, I've given it a lot of thought and I don't think it's a good idea for you to be in class with kids older than you," Rose informed.

"What are you getting at?" Ginnie questioned.

"Well, since I need you at home and you are so far ahead in your studies we're not going to enroll you in school. You'll stay home and help with Gil and Maggie."

"But, mother, I want to go to school."

"No use whining about it. Me and your father have made the decision."

"He's NOT my father. He's just your husband. NOT my father," Ginnie protested defiantly.

"I don't want to hear that kind of talk," Rose responded sternly.

"I just don't understand why you even like him after he did whatever it was that Momma said he did to you."

"That'll be just about enough of that crude talk out of you, young lady," Rose snarled.

"But, Mama . . ."

"No buts about it. Just be quiet and you can put school out of your mind. You'll be staying home to help with your brother."

"But, Mama. . . !"

"Don't talk back, young lady. You'll do as you're told."

Ginnie felt that her life had crashed, but the dutiful daughter protested no further. She remained at home and continued her role as caregiver to her younger siblings when other children went off to school.

Still disappointed that no soldiers or Indians ever showed up at Fort Concho, a move from the old officer's quarters to a real house in another part of town pleased Ginnie. In late September, the family moved to a modest frame home on West Fourteenth Street. The freshly painted structure appeared as a storybook cottage to the young girl and she hoped that easier times with fewer chores lay ahead. For a few weeks, Rose did shoulder more responsibility for household chores, but Ginnie remained as the one who bathed, diapered, and performed many motherly tasks for baby Gil.

The forlorn young girl missed the colorful foliage that beautified the landscape in and around Denison each fall. The normally pleasant season seemed more like winter to her as northerly winds penetrated the house on West Fourteenth Street. Loose windows and doors allowed entry of autumn's chilly breezes into the structure. During December and into January those cold blasts of air turned to frigid winter winds that howled like a freight train across the barren landscape. Record snowfall and subfreezing temperatures that plagued the area in January and February of 1930 made life almost unbearable for Ginnie and Maggie. Each night they snuggled close under several layers of quilts as protection against the bone-chilling drafts that swept through the old house. The elder sister did not recall a more miserable season than the one she now experienced. *I bet Momma and Papa aren't freezing to death like we are,* Ginnie thought as she longed for the warmth of the fire in the ornate cast iron wood-burning stove with shiny chrome trim at her grandparent's house.

As winter descended on San Angelo, Rose put many additional chores on Ginnie and it seemed to the daughter that her mother spent more time in bed than normal. Day after day and night after night, nerve-wracking hacking and coughing emanated from the mother's bedroom and the daughter became frightened. Most morning's she stripped blood-soaked sheets and pillow cases from her mother's bed. Sometimes the spells lasted for what seemed like hours and Ginnie's concern grew as the doctor who had assisted in Gil's birth made daily visits to the home.

On February 17, 1930, Ginnie realized that the coughing spells had ceased and she hoped that her mother felt better, but as Allen emerged from the room in tears she knew that Rose had gone to be with Jesus. Just as they did with her father, men in dark suits came and carried her mother away.

Ginnie's teeth chattered and she shivered from the cold blustery north wind and the light dusting of snow that caused the discomfort, but it held no comparison to the grief that filled her soul. Allen pushed a baby carriage with little Gil inside as he, Ginnie, and Maggie stood on the platform at the train depot. They watched as the same men in dark suits loaded a casket that contained the earthly remains of the wife and mother into a box car. The train carried the body and the family back to Denison where Rose Lee Wentworth Hilton Gentry found her final resting place in the Oakwood Cemetery.

CHAPTER 2

THE FORMATIVE YEARS

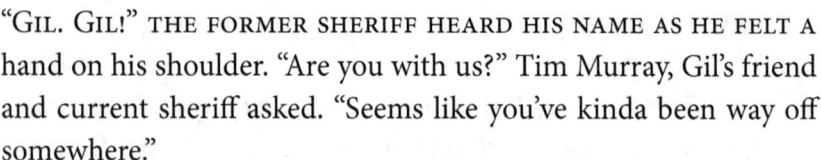

"GIL. GIL!" THE FORMER SHERIFF HEARD HIS NAME AS HE FELT A hand on his shoulder. "Are you with us?" Tim Murray, Gil's friend and current sheriff asked. "Seems like you've kinda been way off somewhere."

"I reckon I was," Gil responded. "You ready to blow this joint? I gotta get back to the car and get me some oxygen." In his waning years the old lawman depended on oxygen from a portable bottle when away from the house, and a concentrator at home. He left the small container that helped him breathe in the car out of a sense of pride. He did not want many folks around him informed of his infirmities.

"Boy, you sure were far away," Sheriff Murray noted as they walked through the massive prison gates and headed to the parking lot.

A full moon and bright stars illuminated the clear Colorado sky as Gil Gentry and Sheriff Tim Murray traveled the steep. crooked mountain highway toward home. Although Gil engaged in conversation during the two-and-one-half hour trip from Colorado State Penitentiary in Canon City back to Leadville, he still seemed melancholy and far away to the current sheriff. He noted a single tear that ran down his old friend's face.

"Thinking about Marcia and the horror she suffered, and how long it took for Herron to get what was coming to 'im?"

"Yeah, some. I'll never get that out of my head, but actually I was questionin' what the hell made me become a lawman in the first place, and have to deal with scum like Herron," Gil replied. "I was thinkin' about my family, my birth, and my mother's death."

"You might remember your family, but I don't reckon you remember the day you were born," Murray noted with a chuckle.

"Nah, I just remember the stories I was told, mostly by my sister, Ginnie. I really think my turbulent childhood and troubled young adult life in some weird way caused me to turn to law enforcement. My father wasn't real good to me. Sometimes he was downright mean, and as a young kid I cried myself to sleep a lot of nights wondering why somebody, anybody, didn't help me. I always kinda figured that he blamed me for my mother's death and that's probably why he treated me like he did."

"What makes you think that?" Murray questioned.

"From what Ginnie told me, mother never really recovered from the trauma she endured while givin' me life and she died nine short months later, so he figured it was my fault."

"Seems to me it was more his fault. He was the one what got her pregnant."

"Sis told me that my grandmother, Momma Wentworth, blamed my father. Momma insisted if Mom had been close where family could have taken care of her, she wouldn't 'a died. Who knows? Seems like there was plenty of blame to go around."

"One thing is for sure, it was not your fault. You being a lawman probably had nothing to do with your father, your mother's death or your childhood, old man. It was just meant to be."

"Nope, I started thinkin' about it as a young man. Don't really know why, but somehow, I thought if I was some kinda cop I might be able to make a difference for kids that were raised like I was. Also, being the lazy kid that I was, I thought it'd be a kinda easy job."

"Well, we both know that ain't so," Murray responded.

"Yeah, when I first started as a deputy we worked six days a week, and not eight-hour days, but twelve."

"It ain't quite that bad nowadays, but close."

"Sometimes in the winter we'd get two days off, but that didn't help much. With all the snow and ice around here, all you could do was hole up in the house. With only one day off in summer, where the hell could you go and do anythin'?"

"So, you found out it wasn't easy, but you stayed with it."

"Yep, I did. I believe it was my upbringin', my restless life, and finally a good woman that made me stick it out. Without her I would have most likely kept on in my wanderin' ways. Probably would have wound up dead or in prison myself," Gil insisted.

"But you were already sheriff when you met Katy," Murray reminded. "I might add, you did make a big difference in her kids' lives."

"Yeah, I was already sheriff, but I still had itchy feet. Had nothin' to keep me in one place or on the same job. I was a wanderer. Needed to see what was beyond the next mountain. Still do, but after I've ventured over the next summit I'm always ready to get home to Katy," Gil informed. "Damn, I'm a lucky man havin' the best woman in the world waitin' for me at home."

"You're right about that. I've often wondered how she put up with the likes of you all these years," Murray noted with a smile.

* * *

As a young child, Gil felt lost. He had no memory of his mother, since she had died when he had only reached the age of nine months, and his father did not give him the attention that he so desperately craved. His two grandmothers, Momma Wentworth and Ida Gentry, devoted much of their time to the boy. The maternal grandmother loved the baby dearly, but the care of

Ginnie and Maggie dominated her efforts. Gil spent most of his childhood years in the home of his widowed Grandma Gentry.

Gil's muddled mind blocked out much of his young life and the early years seemed no more than a blurred dream to him until Christmas Day in the year 1944. Like many Christmases in North Texas, the sun shone brightly, and the still atmosphere made for a beautifully warm yuletide. That unforgettable day filled with tensions and hurtful words burned deep into the fifteen-year-old boy's mind. His father Allen's brother, Ken, also lived in their mother's home and numerous other family members joined them and Gil for the annual Christmas feast prepared by Ida Gentry. The woman had worked hard for several days, cooking many of her children's yuletide favorites. Scrumptious aromas of turkey and dressing filled the room and the tantalizing smell of pumpkin pie that baked in the oven drifted through the air while the group passed the delicious dishes around the table. Tension filled the room when an argument broke out between Ken and another brother, Vern, who it seemed was just itching to stir up a fight.

"Ken, there's something been bugging me for a long time. I can't hold it back any longer."

"What the hell are you gettin' at?" Ken questioned.

"Seems to me that you and Allen are takin' unfair advantage of Mom, livin' here free of rent, lettin' her cook for you, do your warshin', and such. Just isn't right," Vern asserted.

"Vern has a point," their sister Merle chimed in. Their two other sisters just continued with their feast as the brothers engaged in snarly comments back and forth.

Ken's response resonated in young Gil's mind and remained etched there for a lifetime. "You don't know what the hell you're talkin' about. I haven't seen you out there in the kitchen givin' her a hand. You and the rest of your bunch just come waltzin' in here and scarf down a free meal without so much as a 'thank you'. Besides,

17

I'm takin' care of Mom. It's Allen and that no-good boy of his that make life hard for her. Brought the result of his dilly-dallyin' here and dumped the lazy little bastard on her. Shoulda kept his pants zipped and none of this woulda happened."

"Please don't be talking like that," Ida implored quietly. "There are women and kids at the table and they don't need to be hearing such."

"Hold on just a damn minute, Ken," Allen, who had an extremely hot temper, interrupted as he slammed a bowl down on the table with a crash that sent mashed potatoes and slivers of glass flying. "Who goes to work every day and brings a paycheck to the house? It sure as hell isn't you. You just live here scot-free and never contribute one damn dime. And you've got the nerve to call Gil no good and lazy?"

"Don't matter how much money you bring in. It don't compare to her puttin' up with that lazy bas . . . sorry, Mom. The lazy bum just hangs around the house and don't do nothin' to help out," Ken retorted.

Wham! Allen's chair fell backwards and hit the floor as he jumped up, grabbed Ken by his collar, and shouted, "Let's just go out back and settle this."

"Boys, please. It's Christmas."

Vern, who enjoyed a good fight, especially between his two brothers, followed as they ignored their mother's pleas and stormed out the back door. Ida arose from the table, wiped tears from her face, and spoke in her normally calm manner, "I'm feeling a bit tired and I can't abide seeing my boys fighting. I'm going to my room and lay down for a spell."

Allen and Ken headed to the back yard where they intended settlement of their dispute by physical means. Vern trailed several feet behind his brothers, since he desired no physical involvement in the confrontation that he had stirred up. The role as a witness was as close as he got to the confrontation. Ida went to her bedroom and the remaining family members continued their meal. The seemingly uncaring group paid little attention to the fist fight that took place outside, and they thought nothing of the exhaustion of the family matriarch. It seemed to young Gil that nobody cared about the fracas between his father and uncle or the wellbeing of his grandmother. He did not know how to react, so he just sat stunned and silent.

Whap! Whap! Gil heard the slam of fist against face as the scuffle continued. He wondered how the rest of the family carried on with their meal while the melee out back cranked up into full swing. The boy figured they would just keep eating even if his father and uncle killed each other. A pained moan that emanated from Ida's bedroom caught the attention of the teenager. The diner's continued consumption of the repast with little regard to the altercation between Ken and Allen or the low groans from an adjoining room.

"Somethin's wrong with Grandma," Gil shouted at his father and uncles out back.

Intensely embroiled in the confrontation, the father and uncle ignored the boy.

"Can you two stop actin' like a couple of thugs and see what's wrong with Grandma?" Gil asked sharply.

"Boy, don't take that tone with me, less you want a whoopin'," Allen replied.

"Whoop me if you want to. Won't be nothin' different, but do it after you check on Grandma," the grandson who had endured many whippings demanded.

Ken wiped blood from his busted lip on his shirt sleeve as the fighting came to a halt and Allen responded. "What do you mean somethin's wrong?"

"She's groanin' somethin' fierce. Sounds like she's hurtin' real bad." Gil answered.

Allen, Ken, and Vern passed by the rest of the family in the dining room who continued their meal. They ran to their mother's room where they found her clutching her chest and writhing in pain.

"Something's bad wrong," the woman muttered weakly as she gasped for breath. "My chest hurts something fierce, my left shoulder and arm are paining me terrible, I feel like a elephant is sitting on my chest, can't breathe, and my jaw even hurts."

Phone service had not come to the Gentry household, so at his father's instructions, the extremely frightened Gil ran like a man possessed to the nearest telephone in the neighborhood and called the doctor. The caring physician immediately left his own Christmas celebration and headed to the Gentry house.

"I'm sorry, but I got here too late," the doctor informed as he emerged from Ida's bedroom. "She was already gone. Her heart just stopped."

My dad and my uncles. That's what killed her, Gil thought as he wiped away tears from his face. *All that fightin' they do all the time. Just too much for Grandma. Oh, God. What am I gonna do without her?*

Unlike the sunshine of Christmas Day, gray clouds that hung low in the sky and raw winds that whistled through the trees added an air of gloom to the cold late December morning when the family gathered at Fairview Cemetery. There Ida Gentry found her final resting place. As men in dark suits lowered the casket into the deep, dark hole, young Gil knew that his life had changed forever. The grandmother whom he loved had filled the role as his mother and protector. She had constantly intervened between the boy and his father who exercised strict disciplinarian action that some considered abuse.

* * *

"The woman was a saint," Gil muttered quietly as a tear trickled down his cheek. "The woman was a saint."

"What did you say?" Murray questioned.

"What?" Gil asked. "Did I say somethin'?"

"You were mumbling about some woman being a saint."

"Oh, I reckon I did. Thought I was just dreamin'. If ever a saint walked this earth, it was my grandmother Gentry. Never heard an angry word come from her mouth. Most carin', laid-back, and easy-goin' person I've ever known. Just don't know how she always stayed so calm with my father and his stupid brothers, actin' like a bunch of hoodlums."

"Why the tear, my friend?"

"You weren't supposed to see that."

"But, I did," Murray replied. "You want to tell me about it?"

"I was just rememberin' the day she died," Gil answered sorrowfully. "I think bein' so mild-mannered helped kill her. She just let my father and his brothers walk all over her. If she had spoken out, not bottled things up inside, and said what she thought maybe they would have acted better and she might not have passed when she did. I believe she died from a broken heart. That's when my life really started downhill. That woman meant everythin' to me, but she died and left me at the mercy of my mean, sadistic father."

* * *

After the death of his beloved grandmother, Gil Gentry felt lost and alone, even though he shared a home with his father and uncle. The Gentry brothers argued often over things that really did not matter and many times those disputes resulted in physical resolution in the backyard. As young Gil witnessed those altercations, his confusion about adults and life in general grew. His grandmother had lived peaceably while his male role models exhibited examples of violence as resolutions for problems, big or small. Under the guise of discipline, the father often exacted harsh physical punishment on the boy.

As the son grew more rebellious and Allen became less tolerant over the next couple of years, many confrontations occurred between father and child. Young Gil had cultivated friendships with several older ne'er-do-well boys who consumed a lot of beer, enjoyed street racing in their old jalopies, constantly pursued the physical favors of many young women, and generally raised hell. Numerous times Gil accompanied his buddies as they ventured across the Red River into Oklahoma for the purchase of beer, wine, or hard liquor. The proprietors of the beer joints cared little about the ages of the boys since they added income to his already lucrative business. Many folks from dry Grayson County, Texas made the trek into Bryan County, Oklahoma and purchased the potations. Young Gil learned about life from "working girls" who operated in back rooms of the establishments. Many of the loose, perverted women waived the normal fee in exchange for the excitement of relations with a good-looking, hormonally charged teen-ager.

It seemed to the extremely inebriated Gil as he entered the house after one of the trips across the river, that the screen door screeched so loudly and the deafening creak of the old floor boards woke the dead, and probably his father. All hell broke loose when Allen flipped the light switch and exposed the drunken boy who had collapsed on the davenport.

"Boy, you been across the river again with that bunch of no-goods?" Allen shouted suspiciously as Gil arose from the couch and stumbled through the house toward his room.

"What if I have? What's it to you?" Gil responded as he turned and faced his angry father.

Whap! The sound echoed through the night when Allen backhanded the boy as he screamed. "DON'T SASS ME, BOY. Won't have a no-good, stupid son of mine comin' in at all hours drunker 'n Cooter Brown. Won't have you hangin' around with that good-for-nothin' bunch."

"They're my friends. They care a hell of a lot more about me than you do."

Whap! Whap! Allen backhanded the boy repeatedly and knocked him to the floor. "I'll teach you to come in all soused up and talkin' to me like that."

"All I ever wanted was your love and approval," Gil blurted out when his true feelings emerged from his mouth as he picked himself up and glared at his father. "Just seems like you don't really give a damn about me."

"Don't you dare talk to me like that," Allen screamed.

"I'll talk to you any damn way I want to, old man," Gil shouted.

"There just isn't any talkin' to you when you're like this. Get your sorry ass to your room. We'll settle this in the mornin' when you're sober."

* * *

"All I ever wanted was your love," Gil mumbled. "All I ever wanted. . ."

"Gil, you're mumbling again," Sheriff Murray informed.

"Sorry. I was just thinkin' about my dad and the way he treated me, especially after my grandma died."

* * *

Seventeen-year-old Gil heard little of what the teacher said as he sat in a classroom at Denison High School. The boy stood taller and was a year older than his classmates, having failed in his studies in an earlier year, but lack of intelligence had not contributed to the failures. The extremely smart boy never concentrated on studies, but instead he fantasized about faraway places.

Too damn pretty outside to be cooped up in here, Gil thought as he gazed out the window and daydreamed. *I need to see what's in the next county and in other states. Ain't really nothin' here for me. I'll go crazy if I spend one more day behind these walls. Gotta get out of this school and this hick town. Life's waitin' out there somewhere for me and I've got to find it.*

The next several days Gil did not attend classes, he left the house at the usual time, but he did not head to school. He ran the streets of Denison and made numerous trips across the river with his friends. After a couple of weeks Allen figured out his son's errant behavior and all hell broke loose once again in the Gentry household.

"You no-good, lazy son-of-a-bitch, I know what you've been up to. Goin' across the river with that bunch of scum you hang out with, gettin' drunk, and cavortin' around with those loose women in the back rooms," Allen screamed when he returned to the house earlier than normal and found Gil at home when he should have been in class.

"How do you know about them 'loose' women?" Gil questioned sarcastically.

"Never you mind about that," Allen replied sheepishly. "Why in God's name have you not been goin' to school?"

"I can't stand being cooped up and listenin' to those teachers babble on and on about useless stuff that don't mean a hill of beans to me."

"Don't you want to get an education and have some smarts?"

"That bunch 'a old maids they call teachers don't know nothin' about livin'. I've got to see the world and have me some fun doin' it," Gil replied.

"Here's the deal, Mr. Smarter Than Your Teachers, you have three choices: get your butt back in school, get yourself a job, or join the army. You're not gonna lay around all day, run the streets, or get drunk with your buddies. I won't have it," Allen informed. "Now what's it gonna be?"

"Anythin' to get away from you and this stinkin' town, old man. I reckon I'll join up."

And so young Gil Gentry became a soldier when Allen accompanied him to the recruiter's office, since at age seventeen the military required parental consent. The young, restless soul had at last escaped the hick town and the fury of his abusive father.

* * *

"How'd it go in the Army?" Murray inquired.

"Not too good at first, but I adjusted," Gil answered. "I started to feel like I belonged to somethin' and not so alone like I did at home. Those years in service passed pretty damn quick. Spent some time in Korea and Japan. It was a dangerous time in dangerous places, but I never woulda got to see those countries if I hadn't joined up."

"What did you do after your tour of duty ended?"

"Worked for a while drivin' a loggin' truck up in Oregon, but after awhile I thought I'd give home another chance."

"How'd that go?"

"I still didn't really fit in. Me and Dad lived with Momma Wentworth for a while after she broke her leg and needed help. Papa Wentworth had gone to his glory. She was real good to me, but I needed more, you know, independence. I always had law enforcement in the back of my mind, and, as dumb as it sounds, I wanted to make a difference, maybe in some kid's life. I worked as a fireman for a while at the Denison Fire Department and tried to get on with the Denison Police Department, but for some reason they didn't want me."

"How'd you wind up out here in Colorado?" Murray asked.

"Read about the Climax Mine where they mined mollybedam . . . uh, molybdenum, however the hell you say it. Some kinda stuff they put in steel to make it harder. I'd heard about gold and silver minin' in Colorado, but not that other stuff. Anyhow, they needed truck drivers and I had experience from my loggin' days so I headed west. You pretty much know the rest."

As the hum of the engine and the rumble of road noises lulled Gil to sleep his thoughts turned from his distant past to the situation that brought him to the current event. He had dealt with many crimes and criminals in his career, but none so horrific as the brutal rape and murder of Marcia Leggett by the disgusting scumbag, Richard Herron.

CHAPTER 3

THE NEW SHERIFF

At Gil's insistence, his nephew Randy had come from his home in Texas for a visit with the uncle whom he loved dearly and respected deeply. The more adamant than normal request had seemed somewhat mysterious, but the nephew enjoyed his times with his uncle, so he dropped everything and readily accepted the invitation. Unfortunately, Randy's wife, Barbara, could not schedule time off from her job, so he traveled alone. He feared revelation of some kind of bad news, since Gil had almost reached his eightieth year and his health had deteriorated. The nephew knew that disclosure of his uncle's motives would come only when the elder felt it necessary.

The old man told Randy many stories about his life, but that did not seem out of the ordinary. He began with a tale of how he landed in Colorado and ended up as sheriff. Randy had often wondered about those circumstances.

"You listen real good, boy. Remember the stories I'm a-tellin' you. Take notes if you need to," the uncle instructed. The declaration seemed odd to the nephew.

"Yes, sir," Randy acquiesced.

"Good! Now let me tell you about becomin' sheriff of Lake County."

"I bet it was a quite a shock moving from Denison, Texas to Leadville, Colorado,"

"Hell, yeah it was. Comin' from the gentle rolling countryside to the land of majestic mountains, high valleys, and thin air," Gil replied.

"Thin air?" Randy questioned. "What are you talking about?"

"Hell, boy. You oughta know what I mean. Ever' time you come for a visit I see you gaspin' for breath, especially for the first few days until you get acclimated to the lack of oxygen in these high altitudes."

"Oh, yeah. I see what you mean."

"I'd been in some mountains when I was loggin' up in the Northwest, but I didn't pay much attention to how big they were. This here country was a totally new experience. The way of life in Leadville was real foreign to what I was used to, but I had me a good job at the Climax, I'd left that hick town in Texas behind, and I no longer had to deal with my Dad."

* * *

So that's the place I'll be workin' out of, Gil thought when he drove past the Climax Mine as he headed south on Highway 24 on his way to Leadville. *Pretty big and impressive. Probably the biggest employer hereabouts. It was a stroke of luck, landin' a job with 'em.*

Got to find me a place to live in town. Can't afford to stay at the Silver King Inn too long. Need somethin' more permanent and real cheap, the traveler pondered as he checked in to the only motel in town.

Leadville, Colorado, appeared smaller and more "hickish" than Gil's hometown and he wondered if he had made a serious error. Prospects for living accommodations in the quaint little town seemed slim to the young man from the flatlands of Texas. As he drove down Harrison Avenue he observed no apartment buildings and even the hick town of Denison had one or two rental establishments. The small residential areas that lay to the east and west of the main drag appeared fully occupied, but that did not matter since he only needed a room with a bath and a kitchenette. The newcomer thought maybe he should have checked into the availability of rental property before he accepted the job. Discouraged and hungry, Gil stopped at the first café he spotted, the Golden Burro Café and Lounge.

"Haven't seen you 'round before," the waitress noted. "What can I get you to drink?"

"Bring me a Coors," Gil replied.

"Coors it is. The special tonight is chopped steak, baked potato, and salad. Only $1.25."

"Sounds good, but a little high priced. Oh, well. Go ahead and bring me one of those."

"Whatcha doing in these parts?" the waitress asked when she delivered the beer.

"Got me a job drivin' a truck for the Climax," Gil answered. "Don't look like there's no place to rent a room hereabouts. You know of anythin'?"

"It ain't much," she replied. "but I heard they got rooms for rent at the old Delaware Hotel. Some outfit bought the place a few years back and intended to turn it into apartments, they was callin' 'em condominiums, but that didn't pan out so they're rentin' out rooms. The place is kind of a flop house, but they say some of the rooms even have their own bathroom, a fridge, and a hotplate."

"Sounds perfect," Gil declared. "Got me a room at the Silver King for tonight, but I'll check on, . . .what was the name of the place again?"

"The Delaware Hotel. Used to be a real nice place back in Leadville's heyday. Just across the street and down about a block. Sits on a corner. Can't miss it."

* * *

"And that's when I started livin' at the Delaware," Gil related. "She was right. The place was a dump, but I didn't care long as I had a bed to sleep in, along with a place to take a bath and take care of other business."

"And you were still living there in seventy-nine?" Randy questioned.

"Yep. Stayed there 'til me and Katy got hitched. Got me one of the rooms with its own bathroom, a fridge, and a hotplate. That's all I needed. Besides, there wasn't any other places around. Had no choice."

* * *

"Last door down the hall to the right on the second floor," the agent said as he handed Gil the key to his new home.

The old stairs sounded plumb ghostly as they creaked and groaned loudly in the dark stairwell when Gill ascended to the second floor of the old Delaware Hotel. *Click, screech, screech,* the door announced his arrival when he inserted the key, turned the lock, and pushed the barrier open. The room obviously had not been occupied in years since the musty smell of dust and grime almost choked the new tenant. He immediately crossed the room, opened the one and only window in the main space, and the opening revealed a bird's eye view of downtown Leadville along Harrison Avenue.

When Gil opened the only other door in the room he observed a less than desirable space the rental agent had touted as a nice private bathroom. The old clawfoot tub that sat underneath a full-length window looked grungier than any he had ever seen. *I'll have to cover that there window with somethin', less I want all of*

Leadville to get a show when I take a bath. That'd give folks a real good impression of the newcomer, he mused as he took a gander at the toilet that appeared worse than the tub. A small smoked-up mirror hung above a dingy off-white-colored sink that stood opposite the other fixtures.

The next morning Gil knocked over a lamp that sat on a small night table as he pulled himself up out of the old bed. The thing sagged so badly toward its middle that he felt as though he had slept in a cocoon. It did not stand on its own, but stood propped against one wall in the main room. A rickety old chair sat by the window that looked out over Harrison Avenue. A small refrigerator and a table topped by a greasy hotplate graced the remaining wall. The tenant hung his few shirts, a couple pair of Wranglers, and his heavy coat on a clothes rod that stretched across one corner of the room as a makeshift closet. Gil cared little about the dilapidated condition of the place. He had a roof over his head, a place to sleep, a tub for a bath, a pot to piss in, and cooking facilities. What more could a man ask for?

* * *

"The place sounds pretty disgusting to me," Randy asserted.

"I reckon it was," Gil responded. "But what the heck did I care. I had a fridge for my Coors and everythin' else I needed. Besides, over the years I scrounged up some better furniture, cleaned the place up a bit, and made it tolerable."

"Maybe tolerable to you, Gil," Katy interjected. "but when we moved your stuff out of there after we married I found it grimy and 'intolerable.'"

"Yeah, but, darlin', you're a woman and women are more persnickety about such things than us guys. Ain't that right, Randy?"

"If you say so, Uncle Gil."

"Besides, darlin', that's just another one of them ways you turned this old heathen into a decent human bein'."

* * *

Kinda reminds me of that beer joint across the river from Denison where I used to go with my ne'er-do-well buddies. Sure caused a bunch of fights between me and my old man, Gil thought as he guzzled down a beer while he sat on a bar stool with his feet propped on the brass foot rail at the Silver Dollar Saloon. The historic bar located near the south end of Harrison Avenue and well within walking distance of the Delaware became Gil's favorite hangout. He frequented the joint most days after work.

"Buy me a beer, stranger?" a bleached blond gal asked as she sidled up to Gil.

"Sure thing," he answered.

"Where'd you come from? Started noticing you coming in a couple a weeks back."

"Came out from Texas to work at the Climax," he replied.

"You looking for a good time?" She asked as she placed her hand on Gil's knee and move it up his leg.

"Don't mind buyin' you a beer and I enjoy the conversation, but if you mean what I think you mean by a 'good time', no offense, ma'am, thanks, but no thanks."

"Well, that's sure different," she replied as she jerked her hand away from Gil's thigh. Most guys what come in here are ready, willing, able and raring to go."

"Hope you don't take no offense, ma'am, but that just ain't me. Used to be, but no more."

"Oh, no offense taken. It's kinda nice just talking to a gentleman that ain't expecting nothing more."

Many encounters took place regularly with other girls, but Gil, although lonely, had no interest in the women. He had experienced what they offered in back rooms at the beer joints across the river from his hometown. The man still had what he called "itchy feet," the desire to know what lay beyond the horizon remained strong, but when it came to women and relationships, he had gained a level of maturity. At this point in his life he hoped for a more serious and permanent bond with a decent woman. Prospects looked slim in Leadville. Gil had no idea that a life-changing connection lay several years down the road in the mountain town.

* * *

"Proves what a decent guy you are," Randy remarked.

"I wasn't always that strait-laced," Gil responded. "And Katy knows it. She's the one what made a decent human bein' out of me. Made me a 'real' man."

"Did the bleached blond keep coming on to you?" Randy questioned.

"No, but we actually became pretty good friends. We just sat at the Silver Dollar, drank a few beers, and talked. She wasn't the marryin' kind so nothin' ever came from it."

"Darn good thing too," Katy added with a chuckle.

* * *

Oh, crap, Gil thought as his ore truck slid across the snow and ice-covered Highway 24. *Drivin' this thing is a bigger chore than I figured. It was okay so long as the weather was good, but I never drove in this kind of stuff when I was loggin' since production got shut down when winter came on. Reckon I shoulda put them chains on like they told me.* The vehicle swerved and skidded across the oncoming lane and finally came to rest against a grove of trees on an incline beside the two-lane road. Had the mishap taken place just a few hundred feet further down the crooked narrow highway, the truck with Gil inside would have gone off the edge. It would have plunged several hundred feet down into a ravine in an area where no trees blocked the steep mountainside.

Good God. I coulda been killed, he thought as he sat, stunned. His head hit against the steering wheel on impact and a large gash gushed blood. The flow of red stuff ran down his face and into his eyes. *Workin' for the Climax is a damn good job, but I'm not sure it's worth the risk.*

"Come in, dispatch," Gil requested weakly on his radio. "Got a problem here."

"Yeah, this is dispatch. You don't sound too good. What's the problem?"

Gil explained his predicament. "Slid off the road. Landed against a bunch of trees."

"You okay?"

"Not really. Got blood runnin' down my face and I feel plumb queasy."

"Don't move. Just sit still and stay where you're at."

"Got to get out of the truck. There's smoke comin' out from under the hood."

"Yeah, you'd best get away from it. I'll call the sheriff, he'll be out there shortly, and he'll have an ambulance come out too."

"Hell, don't need no ambulance. Just a little cut."

"Ambulance on its way."

Gil exited the vehicle, walked around to the front where he noted extensive damage and two shredded tires. The injured man left a bright red trail of blood as he stumbled across the snow until he reached a distance where he felt safe. Flames and smoke billowed out from under the hood of the truck as Gil sat down in the snow. *Varoom!* The truck exploded, flames leapt skyward, and clouds of dark smoke filled the air. The driver fell unconscious. While he drifted in and out of consciousness, Gil heard sirens as the emergency vehicles approached.

"Sir, are you okay?" Gil heard a voice as it questioned from somewhere in his fogged-up mind.

"Yeah, I'm fine. Just a little scratch," he answered.

"A little scratch, my eye. It's huge gash and it's pouring blood out like a fire hydrant. The paramedics are here. They'll take care of you."

* * *

"I don't remember much until after they got me to the hospital. I was real woozy and kept driftin' in and out," Gil informed.

"Sounds like you were worse off than you thought," Randy noted.

"It was pretty bad, took a bunch of stiches to put me back together, but things got worse before they got better. Not my injuries, but other problems."

"What are you talking about?" Randy questioned.

"I'll get to it," Gil answered. "First thing I remember at the hospital was hearin' that same voice in my foggy mind that asked me if I was okay."

* * *

"Sir, can you tell me what happened?" The familiar voice asked.

"Truck just started slidin' around on the ice and I lost control. Shoulda put them chains on," Gil answered as he opened his eyes and observed the county sheriff at his bedside.

"You are one lucky dude. A little farther down the road and you woulda bought the farm."

"Didn't know the farm was for sale," Gil joked.

"Good to see you've got a sense of humor," the sheriff replied. "Is there somebody I should call for you? Your wife?"

"Thanks, but I ain't got nobody, let alone a wife."

Brian Parker had been the highly respected sheriff of Lake County for many years. Each time he came up for re-election, the extremely well-liked lawman ran unopposed. With only a few exceptions, just about everyone in the county considered the man as a personal friend. A close bond began at that moment as he and Gil experienced an immediate connection that later proved beneficial to the injured truck driver. Unbeknownst to the transplanted Texan, a lifelong friendship had begun that brought a measure of stability to his heretofore unbalanced life.

"Come in and have a seat," Gil's supervisor instructed when the injured employee returned to work.

"What did you want to see me about, Boss?" Gil questioned.

"Gil, I'll get right to the point. Your negligence has caused the company considerable losses."

"What do you mean, my negligence?"

"It's my understanding that you did not put the chains on like you were supposed to. Is that so?"

"I reckon it is," Gil answered.

"Gil, it hurts me to do it, but I've got to let you go. We just can't have folks working for us that don't follow the rules and don't do what they're told."

* * *

"That's what I meant when I told you things got worse. The cut on my head healed, the concussion I got from slamming my head against the steering wheel passed, but losin' my job devastated me."

"I can only imagine," Randy commented.

"I felt like the rug had been jerked right out from under me. Here I was, one thousand miles from home, livin' in a flop house, little money, and no job."

"What did you do?"

"Spent a good bit of time at the Silver Dollar, guzzlin' beer and cryin' on the bleached blonde's shoulder. She was a good listener. I carried a couple of six-packs back to my room most nights. I was a mess until Sheriff Parker rescued me."

* * *

"Gil Gentry, is that you?" Sheriff Parker asked as he walked up to the table where Gil and the bleached blonde sat in the Silver Dollar Saloon. "Man, you look like crap. Worse than you did all cut up in the hospital. What's going on with you?"

"They fired me out at the Climax for not puttin' the chains on my truck. I got no job, very little money, and no prospects," Gil responded.

Apparently, the sheriff saw some potential in the man down on his luck. "You ever consider a job in law enforcement?"

"Strange you should ask," Gil answered. "From the time I was a kid, that's all I ever wanted to do."

"I've got an opening for a deputy. You interested?"

"Damn right I am."

"Get your butt to your room, leave the beer, sober up, get a good night's sleep, get yourself cleaned up, and come see me in the morning," Parker instructed.

Gil relaxed as he soaked in a hot bath before he crawled into bed and slept soundly for the first time in weeks. The prospect of a job as a deputy sheriff fulfilled a lifetime longing, a dream he long figured had no future, might now become a probable reality.

Gil arose early, shaved, donned clean clothes, and the renewed man looked like his old self again when he showed up at the sheriff's office as instructed. "You look a hell of a lot better this morning."

"Thanks, sheriff. I feel a hell of a lot better too."

"Gil, I'm getting close to retirement, a couple of years max, and there really ain't nobody around to take my place. You come to work for me, give it your best, learn the ropes, and as well liked as you are around town, and with my endorsement you'd be a shoo-in for the job. Interested?"

"Damn straight. It's my dream come true."

* * *

"And that's how I became sheriff," Gil explained.

"Parker saw what a good guy you really are," Randy noted.

"Don't know how in the hell he saw anythin' good in that stinkin' drunk sittin' in the Silver Dollar Saloon, but I'm sure glad he did."

"Yeah, and he's still got being a lawman in his blood," Katy injected.

"Right, darlin'. Reckon I'll always be a cop at heart."

"You guys want a cup of java?" Katy questioned as she headed towards the kitchen. "I'll make a fresh pot."

"Sounds good, darlin'."

"Randy, I didn't want to say anything in front of Katy, but did you notice that car that keeps goin' by real slow? Probably some kind a drug deal goin' down."

"I did notice it, but didn't think anything about it."

"Somethin's going on and I'm gonna find out what," Gil informed as he jerked the oxygen tube from his nose, retrieved his service revolver from a drawer, and headed out the door.

"Where is Gil?" Katy asked when she returned.

"Don't know what's going on, but he grabbed his gun and headed out. Said he was gonna find out what's going on with that car that kept driving by real slow."

"Good, Lord," Katy exclaimed. "I told you the cop was still in him."

"Did you catch up to 'em?" Randy asked when Gil returned. "Were they drug dealers, like you thought?"

A sheepish grin came across Gil's face when he answered. "No, they were undercover cops watchin' a house down the street. I always suspected somethin' was goin' on down there. Anyhow, I know one of the cops. Darn good thing too, or they mighta hauled my butt in."

"Good, Lord, Gil. This nonsense has got to stop. You're gonna give me a heart attack. You're not a cop anymore," Katy insisted.

* * *

When Sheriff Brian Parker announced his retirement, no one questioned his replacement. In 1975, the well-liked, hard-working deputy, Gil Gentry, ran unopposed and assumed the office as Sheriff of Lake County Colorado. Only petty crimes took place in Leadville and the new sheriff settled in for a quiet life. Four short years later a horrific crime caused questions in his mind as to his continued career in law enforcement.

CHAPTER 4

THE VICTIM

AFTER NEARLY THIRTY YEARS OF MARRIAGE, KATY GENTRY KNEW her man well. The wife had learned all her husband's personality traits and she realized that after such an emotional experience as a witness to an execution, he would be wound up like a two-dollar watch. The man would be primed to talk the night away when he returned. Gil's nephew from Texas, Randy Hunt, had retired to the guest room several hours earlier and left Katy to wait alone. In anticipation of Gil's frame of mind, she brewed a pot of strong coffee and dozed off as she waited in a recliner by the door.

"Well, Katy, it's finally over and done with," Gil informed when he returned around 3:00AM. He took Katy in his arms, pulled her close in a warm embrace and spoke in soft gentle tones unusual for the normally gruff masculine man, "It don't make me feel much better. I mean, nothin' can make up for what Marcia suffered that night and nothin' can bring her back, but I'm glad it's done."

"I sure hope this brings some closure to her family," Katy responded. "Thirty years is a long time to wait. It must have been a living hell all these years."

"Yeah, her brokenhearted father never got over what happened, and I think that's what finally killed him. Where's Randy?" Gil questioned as his mood lightened somewhat. "Young whipper-snapper couldn't stay awake?"

"Here I am," Randy muttered sleepily as he emerged from the kitchen with a cup of java in his hand. "You guys want a cup?"

"Don't mind if I do," Gil answered.

"Me, too," Katy responded. "You know your uncle. He'll talk all night and we'll need something to keep us awake."

"Like my conversation ain't gonna keep you awake?"

"Now maybe my nightmares will end," Katy remarked.

"I know what you mean, all the testimony and crime scene photos you and the other jurors heard and saw—horrifyin'. One good thing came out of it, though."

"What good could have possibly come out of it?" Randy questioned.

"If Katy hadn't been on the jury and I hadn't been sheriff, we might 'a never got together," Gil declared. He looked at Katy adoringly, reached across the table, and squeezed her hand.

"That's probably true, but what a way to get to know each other," Katy replied as she returned the affectionate gesture.

"I didn't know that's how y'all met," Randy commented.

"Well, actually we had met once before, but only briefly," Katy informed.

"Hell, boy, there's a lot of things you don't know," Gil responded. "That's one reason I insisted that you come for a visit. Especially now."

"What are you getting at?" Randy asked.

"Marcia's story needs to be told. I've read all the books you've written and you're the guy that's gonna tell it. I figured after the execution was the right time for it to be told."

"I appreciate the confidence you have in me, but. . . . "

"No buts, boy. You just listen real close and get it right so people will know that Marcia was a real person, a real flesh-and-blood person, not just a long-forgotten name in a long-ago newspaper article. She was a friend, a sister, and her father's baby girl. You can do that. Make her real and tell the world what happened that ungodly night. Don't hold nothing back. Tell it like it happened."

41

"Since you put it like that, I'll give it my best shot."

"I just wish Marcia's daddy had lived long enough to see justice done," Gil lamented. "He adored that girl."

* * *

Marcia Leggett made her original mark on the family the day she made her appearance into the world, March 17, 1963. The eleventh and last child of Howard and Esther Leggett weighed in at a gigantic ten pounds and she remained somewhat overweight her entire life. The girl's chubbiness made no difference to her siblings or her father, who told her many times, "just more there to love." Marcia's seven brothers and three sisters idolized the latest addition to the family. Fifty-four-year-old Howard adored the child, but Esther considered her as just additional work. A house full of kids to clothe and feed took most of Howard's meager income, but he gave the light of his life, his baby girl, all that he possibly could.

The highly intelligent girl read incessantly. She wrote short stories and poems, mostly from material supplied by the many unusual and funny things that happened in a family with eleven siblings. Marcia possessed a natural way with words. She used the talent as she recounted the sad times, the happy times, and the funny escapades perpetrated by her brothers and sisters. Although smarter than many kids her age the intelligent girl had little interest in school. She dreamed of a life beyond the city limits of Leadville and past the borders of states that surrounded Colorado. Marcia yearned for knowledge of happenings in places like Paris, New York City, or San Francisco—anywhere beyond the horizon.

With the span of years between the Leggett offspring, Marcia experienced separation from several of her siblings before her fifth birthday. The sense of loss she felt each time one of her brothers or sisters moved on with life contributed to her loneliness. She received no affection or attention from her mother, since the woman worked outside the home and showed little interest in her children. The reluctant mother considered her offspring as no more than the results of her husband's unrelenting desires. For the most part, Esther left Marcia's care in the hands of her brothers and sisters. Five of the older ones left the family nest early in her life when they moved away either for career opportunities or marriage. The one most devastating for Marcia was her oldest brother, Erick, who idolized and spoiled her. He remained with the family until the day he received a notice from the local draft board.

"What's the matter?" Marcia questioned as she observed a disconcerting look on Erick's face. The letter in his hand shook as he trembled in anxiety and fear. "What's that letter?"

"It's from the draft board," he answered. "I've been drafted. Got to go for a physical and report for induction next month."

"No! No! Can't be," Marcia sobbed. "I need you here."

"I'm sorry, baby sister, but there ain't nothin' I can do."

The brave young man reported to the military as instructed and served with honor until he lost his life during the Viet Nam conflict. For the rest of her life, Marcia carried memories of the day an army car pulled up and parked in front of the house. The army chaplain brought the bad news, and the loss had a monumental effect on the girl. Until his deployment, Erick had been the big brother that every girl dreamed of. The demise of the sibling who filled the role as Marcia's friend and protector left her devastated with a huge hole in her heart. Although she enjoyed closeness and loved her other siblings, she felt awkward and alone as a teenager. Erick had filled that gap.

Howard Leggett never wavered in his love for the child, even though his heart broke as he realized that the rebellious girl experimented with drugs, alcohol, and sex. Though far from perfect, she remained the apple of her father's eye.

* * *

"You know, Katy, Marcia kinda reminded me of myself, although I was never the apple of my father's eye," Gil noted. "After Grandma Gentry died I felt alone and unwanted. School bored the heck out of me and I always wanted to see what was beyond the horizon, just like she did."

"Could be the similarities is what made the case weigh so heavy on your heart," Katy replied with understanding.

"I reckon that's part of it, but that aside, what Herron did to Marcia had a profound effect on me and a lot of other people."

"Yes, I know," Katy responded. "I'm one of those other people."

"You listenin', Randy? I fixin' to tell you the story."

"I'm all ears," Randy responded sleepily.

"I'll never forget that mornin'. It's like it just happened yesterday," Gil remarked with sadness.

* * *

Clank, clank. The sound of breaking glass echoed through the dark room of the drafty old Delaware Hotel building in downtown Leadville where Gil resided. The annoyed man knocked empty beer bottles off the night table when he reached for the phone that interrupted his sleep as it rang loudly and repeatedly. *What the hell's wrong with people calling at this hour,* Gil thought as he looked through bleary eyes at the old windup alarm clock. *This had better be important, waking me up at four in the morning.*

"WHAT?" he barked as he put the phone to his mouth.

"Hate to bother you at his hour, boss," Deputy Long apologized.

"It damn well better be important."

"It is," Long replied. "We've got a probably rape and attempted murder out by Turquoise Lake."

"Are you drunk? Things like that don't happen in my county."

"No, boss, I'm real sober."

"And what the hell do you mean, 'probable rape'?" Gil snapped. "Either she was raped, or she wasn't. What does she say about it?"

"Haven't talked to her. Two fishermen just came to the station and told me what they found," Long responded. "They're saying that they have never seen anything like this. She's so . . . so messed up, even her own mother wouldn't know her."

"What the hell do you mean, 'so messed up'?"

"Just get your pants on and get your butt out there. It's out on that old road that fishermen use to get to the lake. You know, on the north side of the highway before you get to the lake. I'm heading out there now."

Gil sat up on the side of the bed and groped in the darkness for his Wranglers that lay on a chair close by. He put one leg in the britches, sat down on the side of the bed for a minute, placed his other leg in his pants, pulled them up, zipped the fly, and reached for his socks and boots. The groggy sheriff kicked broken beer bottles aside as he stumbled across the room toward the makeshift closet where he selected a starched and ironed Western shirt. The sheriff pinned on his badge that he retrieved from a bureau that stood on one side of the room and then he strapped his gun on his hip. The number one lawman of Lake County, Colorado was ready for whatever faced him in the dark night . . . or so he thought.

* * *

"Nobody could be prepared for what I saw," Gil spoke softly as he wiped a tear from his ruddy face with a big masculine hand.

"Don't know why you hadn't moved from the Delaware by then," Randy declared, in an effort to change the subject and bring relief to his distressed uncle.

45

"Had no intentions of puttin' down any roots. All I needed was a place to hang my hat, take a shower, and sleep. That shabby old room at the Delaware suited me just fine," Gil replied. "Had no need for a house, but I hadn't yet met Katy. Enough about me. This is Marcia's story."

"You said she was no saint. What did you mean?"

"A lot of folks thought Marcia brought what happened to her on herself with her wild ways, but nobody, I mean nobody, deserves what Herron did to Marcia."

* * *

Marcia's dark, thick, shoulder-length hair that framed her smooth olive-complexed pretty face, and her soft brown eyes caught the attention of many young men, especially that of twenty-five-year-old Richard Herron. He had instantly developed an unhealthy obsession for and had fantasized about what he would do to the sixteen-year-old whom he had seen around Leadville. In hopes of fulfilling that fantasy, he had approached Marcia numerous times. The naïve girl was no stranger to adult activities since she had experienced physical relationships with boys her own age. Although Herron's tall, muscular build sent Marcia's young mind racing to plateaus beyond her experience, she had no interest in older men. Richard's advances seemed to her as only innocent flirtations.

"Let me help you with those groceries," Richard offered as he approached Marcia on the parking lot at the local Safeway store.

"Thanks, I appreciate it," Marcia responded as she eyeballed the tall man's slim muscled torso revealed by the skin-tight tee shirt that he wore. His almost jet-black hair intensified the look in his pensive brown eyes.

"No problem," Richard replied as he placed several heavy bags into the bed of Marcia's old beat-up Ford pickup.

"Haven't I seen you around here before?" the girl questioned.

"Yeah, I live at the RV Park on the road to Turquoise Lake. Buy all my groceries here. Excuse me for being rude, I haven't introduced myself. I'm Richard Herron and you are?"

"Marcia Leggett."

"Well, Marcia Leggett, has anyone ever told you that you have the most beautiful eyes ever? They remind me of a doe. Why don't you come on out to my trailer and we can get acquainted," he suggested as he placed his hand on her arm.

The trusting teenager still did not recognize the lecherous intentions that lurked in the young man's perverted mind. "Some other time. Right now, I need to get home. Got to fix supper for my daddy and brothers and sisters."

* * *

"I can't believe she was that dumb," Randy asserted. "Anybody with half a brain woulda known what he was after."

"The girl trusted everybody, and no man or boy had used such a line on her before. For the most part, she initiated the illicit activities that she engaged in, and the hormonally-charged boys her age eagerly obliged."

"Seems like she was pretty mixed up," the nephew noted.

"That she was," Gil responded. "Richard made a bunch of attempts to lure her out to his trailer, but she never took the bait until that night."

* * *

The Lake County Court House at 505 Harrison Avenue in downtown Leadville, Colorado seemed an unlikely meeting place for the town's teenagers. Like kids in most small towns, they drove up and down the main drag and met up with friends. The courthouse possessed the only parking lot of any size, so it constituted the best possible rendezvous point for the youngsters. For the most part, the teenagers engaged in mostly acceptable activities, and officials looked the other way unless the crowd got too rowdy or they spotted couples that took things a little too far.

The bright moon bathed Leadville in a heavenly light on September 28, 1979, an unusually warm night in the Rocky Mountains. The peaceful town lay cradled in a high valley at over ten thousand feet above sea level surrounded by mountain peaks that towered to fourteen thousand feet. Most residents considered it as an idyllic location, far from big city crime and violence.

"Daddy, I'm gonna meet Linda down at the courthouse and hang out for a while," Marcia informed as she grabbed her purse and truck keys.

"Sweetheart, I wish you'd stay home tonight," Howard implored.

"But, Daddy, it's such a nice warm night and I already told Linda I'd be there."

"Somehow it just don't feel right," the father warned.

"It'll be okay," Marcia responded as she kissed her father on the cheek and then headed out. "You're just an old worry-wart."

Over the objections of her father, Marcia seized the opportunity provided by the warm, moonlit night, jumped in her old Ford truck, and headed to Harrison Avenue

* * *

"Seems like Howard had some kind'a premonition," Randy noted.

"Does look that way," Gil replied. "You know, it's usually mothers that get those kind of feelin's, but Esther appeared uncarin' and had little involvement in her children's lives, so Howard also sorta filled the role as Marcia's mom."

"She should have listened to her daddy," Katy added sorrowfully. "We wouldn't be sitting here talking about it if she had, but most teenagers don't pay much attention to their parents. They think they are invincible and nothing'll happen to them."

* * *

As Marcia pulled her old truck onto the courthouse parking lot, she observed many of her friends who loitered outside their vehicles engaged in teenage chit chat. To her surprise, she spotted her friend Linda standing next to her car accompanied by Richard Herron. Although she had no real interest in the "older" man, a tinge of jealousy crept into her mind when she saw the two together. The twenty-five-year-old appeared totally out of place among the teenaged crowd.

"Hey, Marcia, this is my friend, Richard," Linda announced as Marcia approached the pair.

"Hey, Linda. Hi, Richard," she replied.

"You know Richard?"

"Yeah, I've seen him around town and talked to him a couple of times."

"He's got a job for us. We can pick up a few bucks or get paid with weed," Linda informed.

"What kinda job?" Marcia asked.

"I need somebody to clean my trailer," Richard answered. "Living out there by myself the place gets pretty nasty and I figure you two enterprising girls could do the job. I'll pay you however you like—cash, weed, or anything else you might want."

"Well, does sound kinda interesting," Marcia declared. "How much money or weed or whatever?"

"Why don't we ride out to my place so y'all can see what needs doing? We can figure out what it's worth and how you want to get paid."

The naïve young girls agreed. They climbed into Herron's small red Toyota pickup and headed west out of Leadville on the road that lead to Turquoise Lake, a journey that forever changed their lives.

CHAPTER 5

THE CRIME

HERRON BECAME HIGHLY AROUSED AS MARCIA SAT NEXT TO HIM with her hip and leg against his. He fantasized about his lecherous intent with great anticipation. He, Marcia, and Linda engaged in meaningless chitchat when they headed west out of Leadville. *I'll pay these girls, all right,* he thought. *I'll give 'em somethin' they'll never forget. I'll lure 'em into my trailer 'n then, let the good times roll.*

The Honey Loaf Campground seemed eerily quiet as they drove through the park to where Herron lived in a shabby trailer located at the back, away from vacationers that occupied spaces in the main camping area. The entire episode seemed just a lark to Marcia, but Linda became frightened when Herron's true demeanor surfaced as he approached the dwelling.

"You young ladies sure look real sexy bathed in the moonlight," he stated seductively as he placed one arm around Linda's shoulder and the other around Marcia's waist and pulled the girls close. "Come on in the trailer, we can have a shot of Jack, smoke a joint, get real loose and comfortable, then we can uh . . . discuss the job."

"What do you mean, get comfortable?" Linda questioned as she pulled away from Herron's hold. "Only thing that makes me *un*comfortable is you putting your hands on me and talking like that."

"Oh, Linda come off it," Marcia rebuffed snippily. "He don't mean nothing, just being friendly."

"Just a little drink and a joint to relax," Herron responded. "Be real nice to me and I might give you some of that other stuff that'll make you girls feel real good."

"I don't think I like your kind of relaxing and I got no intentions of being nice to you, the way I think you mean. Just take me back to town," Linda demanded.

Herron realized that Linda's objections had put a damper on his evil intentions. He had originally intended fulfillment of his perverted fantasies with both teenaged girls. The predator knew that successful execution of his deviant plan stood a better chance with Marcia if Linda was out of the way.

"All right, girls. Get back in the truck and I'll take you back to town," he agreed begrudgingly.

Tension filled the air and few words passed between the three as they drove back to Leadville in almost total silence. Herron visualized what he would do to Marcia once he got rid of Linda as the fingers on his right hand tapped the steering wheel incessantly. He showed his agitation with a hateful scowl on his face. Linda remained somewhat frightened, and Marcia figured her big adventure had been spoiled.

* * *

"That doesn't seem too bright to me," Randy asserted. "Taking a ride with a man, nine years their senior and heading to his house, especially at night. Give me a break. Did they really believe he was taking them to his trailer to negotiate a 'job'?"

"According to what Linda told us later when we interviewed her, they felt there was safety in numbers. She said she would not have gone with him by herself, but she wasn't so sure about Marcia," Gil responded. "Marcia was real trusting, kinda reckless, and adventuresome. She was a terrible flirt with the boys, although not normally with older guys."

"I really thought he meant something different than taking Linda back to town when you said he wanted her out of the way," Randy asserted.

"After what happened later with Marcia, it is surprisin' that he didn't get rid of her some other way," Gil responded. "But, if he'd done anything physical to Linda it woulda spoiled his plans with Marcia that he rationalized would be consensual. He'd 'a had to get rid of her too."

"Look, guys," Katy instructed as she peered out the window. "It's snowing real heavy."

A cold chill filled the room as Gil continued, a chill that seemed to Randy as more than that caused by the freezing temperature and snow.

* * *

"I suppose you want me to drop you at your truck too," Herron suggested halfheartedly after Linda got in her car and drove off.

"Yeah, reckon I do," Marcia replied. "It don't feel right going back to your trailer, just you and me."

"Oh, come on, Marcia," he implored as he put his arm around the girl and pulled her close. "We can have a better time without that whiny bitch. I got plenty of Jack and weed back at the trailer, and some of that other stuff, too. I got something else to give you that you'll never forget. We can get high and just do what comes natural."

"I don't think so," Marcia declared as she struggled free from his hold. "I ain't that kinda girl."

"That ain't what I heard," Herron informed. "I heard you're real easy and know how to make those little boys feel like men."

"Not with an old guy like you," Marcia answered sarcastically.

"Now take me to my truck."

"Oh, quit teasing, Marcia. Those boys you been fooling around with ain't nothing. Let a real man make you feel like a real woman. You know you want it."

"Take me back to my truck, NOW!"

"Not 'til I get what I want," Herron answered angrily. "You ain't gonna tease me and then just walk away. We can do this the easy way, and both enjoy it, or we can do it the hard way. Whichever, don't matter to me, but it's gonna happen."

"YOU LET ME OUT OF HERE RIGHT NOW," Marcia shouted as she tugged desperately at the door handle, but Herron had hit the electronic lock button. The terrified girl was trapped. *When we get out of the truck at his trailer, I'll scream,* she thought. *He'll be afraid somebody'll hear me, and he'll let me go.*

"Loosen up, girl," Herron urged. "We're gonna have ourselves a real good time."

"What part of 'no' don't you understand?" Marcia responded. "Now take me back to town."

Marcia knew her escape plan had been spoiled when Herron drove past Honey Loaf Campground and headed up the road toward Turquoise Lake. The panicked teenager screamed at the top of her lungs when Herron parked the truck on a deserted road in a desolate area near the lake. She screamed, kicked at his groin, and clawed at his face as the captor dragged the captive from the cab. He threw her on a mattress in the camper shell on the bed of the pickup.

"Scream all you want to. Makes it more exciting," he instructed as he stood outside the camper, loosened his belt, and unzipped his jeans. "Nobody'll hear you up here nohow. Now you're gonna give me what I want. Relax, girl. You know you want the same thing that I want."

"You let me go," she screamed. "I wouldn't do it with you if you were the last guy on earth."

"You will do it with me, like it or not," the highly agitated pervert screamed as he struck his prey across her face with the back of his hand.

Marcia figured her only chance at escape was through a window on the side of the camper shell that had been broken. The opening seemed just large enough for her exit. The terrified girl kept a close eye on the attacker and when he dropped his pants partway down she figured she could run faster than he could with his britches at his shins. In a desperate attempt at escape, the teenager crawled through the opening and took off in a dead run up over a rise and into a wash. As Herron began the chase he stumbled and tripped over his trousers that lay around his ankles. When the mad man picked himself up off the ground he kicked the offending garment aside and ran after the girl in his jockey shorts. "You're gonna give me what I want or else," Herron shouted as he ran up the rise after her.

There she is, he thought as he reached the top of the rise and spotted the escapee at the bottom of the wash. *I got her now. No way she can run faster than me. She can't get away and I'm gonna have my way with her.*

Unfortunately for Marcia, she tripped over some brush as she started up the opposite side of the gulley, and Herron caught up with her before she stood up. The crazed attacker dove at her feet as she regained her stance and attempted to climb the hill. The white tennis shoes that she wore slipped off her feet as he grabbed them, and the escapee ran free momentarily. As the petrified girl reached the top of the incline, the pursuer grasped her by the legs and the tan pants, already torn and dirty, came off in the struggle. Marcia kicked and fought as Herron pulled her to the ground and ripped off her white underwear. When the attacker released her briefly while he removed his jockey shorts the victim seized the opportunity, jumped up and ran, but the attempt proved unsuccessful. The maniac tossed his undershorts aside, ran after the escapee, tackled her, threw her half naked body to the ground, and climbed on top of her. It seemed to the victim that the horrific act took hours as he brutally raped her. She thought it would never end.

* * *

Gil handed his handkerchief to Katy as he observed a flood of tears that ran down her face. "I'm sorry, darlin'. Didn't mean to upset you. Reckon I've said too much."

"No," Katy responded. "Tell it all so Randy can tell the world. People need to know exactly what happened. Maybe those bleeding-heart liberal idiots will shut up when they know what really happened. You know, that loud-mouthed group that's been protesting the execution."

"I'll relate all the grisly details to Randy, but maybe you shouldn't hear it."

"I don't ever want to forget what happened to that poor girl so go ahead and tell it. I'll be okay. Randy, I'm sorry I got so emotional, but when I was on the jury we saw ungodly crime scene photos and heard all the horrifying details of what happened. A lot more explicit than the way Gil is telling it. They described everything real graphically. I mean *everything*. They didn't leave anything to the imagination. It was awful. I've had nightmares all these years about it."

* * *

His brutal urges finally satisfied, Herron reclined on the ground beside his victim and laughed demonically. His pensive eyes had a cold evil stare and a wild, crazed look covered his face. *This is my chance to get away,* Marcia thought as she observed her attacker, who lay naked in the moonlight with a satisfied smirk, oblivious to her or anything around him. She grabbed her tan pants and headed down into the wash where she searched for her shoes.

"NO, not again," she shouted when she felt Herron's arms around her waist and his body pressed against her as she stood up and pulled at her pants. The horrified girl gained some strength and yanked away from the attacker, her trousers still on the ground. *Whap! Whap!* The back of the madman's hand hit his prey repeatedly until she fell to the earth, where he kicked her, over and over. Herron groaned and became infuriated when Marcia connected her foot to his groin several times with powerful blows. He hit the girl again and again before he pinned his victim to the ground. He sat straddled on top of his target and banged her head against a rock until her body went limp and fell unconscious.

I've killed the bitch, Herron thought as he crawled off her body. *Can't just leave her here for somebody to find. Got to get rid of the body.* The maniac left his seemingly lifeless victim in the wash as he headed back to his truck, parked about fifty feet up the rise. As he approached the vehicle he looked down and realized that his lower body remained exposed. The naked man found his jeans on the ground behind the camper, he pulled them on, reached inside the camper shell, and grabbed a can filled with white gas. *I'll set her on fire and burn her up. If somebody does find her they won't know who she is,* the deranged man rationalized.

Marcia had regained consciousness and when she observed Herron as he stumbled down the hill toward her she lay still in hopes that her attacker, thinking his victim was dead, would leave. A loud cough gave away the ruse as the stench of the accelerant filled the injured girl's nostrils and permeated her lungs when the crazed monster poured the flammable liquid over her battered and bruised body. Marcia felt the gas as it ran down her legs when with one last burst of energy she struggled to her feet.

Oh, hell, she ain't dead, Herron thought when he heard the cough. *Don't matter. She will be after I set her on fire. That's what the bitch gets. We coulda had us a real good time and she'd 'a enjoyed it as much as I did, but no, she had to get all righteous. 'Not that kinda girl,' my ass. Oh, well, I had me a fine time. Best I ever had. Her struggling made it even more exciting.*

Varoom! The gas exploded over Marcia's body when Herron struck a match and threw it on the girl drenched in the liquid, crumpled to the ground.

"Smile," he said cheerfully as he raised a Polaroid camera to his eye. Two flashes, and two photos ejected from the camera, as Marcia writhed and screamed as the flames devoured her hair and skin.

Too bad it turned out this way. She was real fine and the two of us could have had a lot of great times together. Ah, heck. There's a lot of other girls out there just as good or maybe even better. That Linda, now, she's a pretty one. I'll work on her. She'll come around and be next. That Marcia girl got what was coming to her, the demented man thought as he climbed up the hill, got in his truck, and drove away. The evil monster left his victim to die in excruciating pain at the bottom of the gulley next to the lonely road.

* * *

"What a sick bastard," Randy asserted as he absorbed the story. "Execution was too good for him. They shoulda tortured the S-O-B before they stuck the needle to him."

"You gettin' this all down in your brain?" Gil questioned. "You got to write it and make people know she was real."

"Oh, I'm getting it all down, all right, but it's going to be hard for me to write."

"Why? I've read your books and you're good with words."

"Thanks for the compliment, but this is going to be hard. It's out of my comfort zone. I don't write explicit stuff and I don't know how to tell the gritty details without being too graphic."

"You'll figure it out," Gil assured. "You probably need to be a little graphic to make it real."

"Well, maybe, but it still makes me uncomfortable. How did y'all figure out who the perpetrator was?" Randy asked.

"You'll know when I finish tellin' the story," Gil answered. "Can't figure why, but some folks thought there was reasonable doubt, but durin' Herron's last appeal everybody got indisputable evidence of his guilt. The lab over in Denver tested the DNA recovered from her body and from the jockey shorts we found at the scene and from the wet dirt we found next to the area where the fishermen found Marcia. They also tested DNA from a sticky substance we found on some aspen leaves at the cemetery and at the Healy House. It all matched Herron. Those kinds of definitive tests weren't available back in the early eighties."

"What sticky stuff are you talking about?" Randy asked.

"Turned out to be semen."

"How'd semen get there?"

"Hell, boy how do you think it got there? We'll get to that later in the story."

"What do you mean in the 'wet' dirt?"

"Use your imagination, Randy."

* * *

Marcia desperately desired disclosing the identity of her attacker and that, along with sheer determination, kept her alive even after

Herron doused her with gas and set her on fire. The nearly dead victim heard Herron's pickup as he drove away. She struggled, but could not stand. Rocks and greasewood scraped strips of burnt skin and flesh from her naked body as the critically wounded girl crawled up the rise with great difficulty. In excruciating pain, several times she considered just giving up and letting her earthly life ebb away, but she knew she must expose the perpetrator.

The dying girl realized that no traffic traveled the deserted road where Herron had parked his truck. Amazingly, she mustered up the strength and dragged her charred frame one quarter mile toward another dirt lane that led to the main highway. Marcia's battered body could go no further, and she collapsed in the bushes about ten feet to the side of the road used by fishermen for access to the lake. Herron's nearly dead victim passed in and out of consciousness as she lay near the fishermen's lane. The sound of a vehicle as it approached alerted the girl to the possibility that help headed her way. As the headlights drew close she raised up as best she could and waved her skinless arm frantically.

"What's that moving over there in the bushes?" Barry who sat in the passenger seat asked as he and George headed to Turquois Lake for some early morning fishing.

"Good God, Barry, it's a person," George, the driver responded as he slammed on the brakes and brought the car to a stop.

Both men exited the vehicle and ran to Marcia who slumped back to the ground as she thought, *Thank God. Help is here.* At that point, the poor girl slipped back into unconsciousness. The compassionate fishermen realized that something horrific had happened to the bloody, cut-up, half-naked girl. George covered her nakedness with a blanket that he retrieved from the car while Barry sat by the girl and offered what comfort he could.

"We've got to get help," Barry exclaimed. "Let's go back out to the highway and hope a car comes along real soon. We'll tell them what we've found, get them go to Leadville and summon the sheriff and we'll get back to the girl and stay with her until help arrives."

"Maybe one of us should just stay here," George suggested.

"What if whoever did this is lurking in the woods. He might come back and after what he's done to that girl he probably wouldn't hesitate to kill one of us, especially if we're here alone. We've done what we can for the poor girl for now and we won't be gone long."

* * *

"Why didn't they just call the sheriff?" Randy questioned

"Hell, boy. Where is your mind? This happened in 1979. Weren't no cell phones back then, and there weren't no pay phone out there in the sticks."

* * *

Shortly after the two fishermen arrived at the highway, they flagged down a red Toyota pickup with a beat-up camper shell. The two men had no idea that the driver of the Toyota had perpetrated the horrific crime. After they innocently explained the situation to Herron, he offered his assistance. "I'm on my way to work, but I'll stay with the girl long enough for y'all to go get the sheriff."

After they gave Herron vague directions to the girl's location, George and Barry headed into Leadville. They did not realize that they had put the victim in grave danger. "I know the spot," Herron responded. "Y'all go get the sheriff and I'll take care of the girl."

Damn it, why won't that girl die? Herron thought as he figured that she remained in the gulley and mistakenly headed to the lane where he had previously parked the pickup before he committed the crime. *Gotta find her and finish her off before she identifies me.*

The half-crazed monster searched the ravine, trudged up and down each side, but did not locate Marcia. *Where the hell can she be,* he wondered. As he drove around in the darkness in search of his victim, nature suddenly issued an urgent call and the perpetrator stopped his truck near the spot where Marcia lay in the brush.

The girl recognized the sound of the vehicle as that of Herron's Toyota truck, so she lay deadly still. *Please, God. Don't let him find me.* Although he stood only a couple of feet from his victim, the attacker did not see her in the darkness. Marcia held her breath as a stream of Herron's urine splashed on her and puddled near her face. As the madman zipped his pants he thought, *Might as well just give up searching. Don't look like I'm gonna find her nohow. Most likely she'll be dead when they get back.* In desperation, Herron gave up the search and headed into Leadville and north to the Climax mine where he worked.

It seemed odd to Deputy Long and the two fishermen when they arrived at the scene and the man who offered his help had disappeared. A large strip of burned skin filled Long's hand as he checked for a pulse which he found, although it was extremely weak. Nauseated by the incident and the stench of burned flesh, the deputy choked, gagged, and threw up behind a large boulder. He wiped the residue from his mouth as he radioed for an ambulance. The sickened lawman could not be sure, but he suspected that he knew the victim. Marcia's father had solicited his assistance several times when the wayward girl did not come home as expected.

* * *

"That's about the most horrible thing I've ever heard," Randy noted. "You kinda expect stuff like that to happen in Denver, or Los Angeles, or Chicago, you know, the big cities, but here in Leadville?"

"I hadn't lived here too long and had only been sheriff a couple of years when it happened. I'd never heard of such a thing ever happenin' in these parts, and nothin' anyways near like it has happened since," Gil replied.

"Hope it never happens again," Katy added. "It took years for folks around here to get past it, and most never did totally. Maybe now that Herron's dead, people can put it behind them. I sure hope so. I don't ever want to forget Marcia and what happened, but we need to move on as a community.

"Easier said than done in a close-knit town like Leadville," Randy suggested. "Yeah, in a big city maybe, but not here."

* * *

The citizens of Leadville never forgot that horrible night and the horrific crime Herron committed. Gil and his deputies searched for the perpetrator for over a year, and folks in the area lived in fear for the duration. Would the murdering rapist ever be caught? Would he strike again?

CHAPTER 6

THE INVESTIGATION

As Gil pulled out of his parking space at the old Delaware Hotel in downtown Leadville, he observed a red Toyota pickup with a beat-up white camper shell when it ran a red light at a high rate of speed. *Only one signal light in Leadville and that idiot has to speed through it. He's a real lucky guy,* the sheriff thought. *Any other time I'd stop him, and he'd get a ticket with a stiff fine. Might even hauled his butt in and let him cool his heels in the slammer overnight, but I've got a more pressin' issue right now.* The sheriff of Lake County, Colorado did not realize that a murdering rapist just passed in front of him and avoided capture.

Irritated that he did not have time for apprehension of the speeder, Gil headed west out of Leadville toward Turquois Lake and the crime scene. *It's horrible that that poor girl got raped, but at least she's alive,* the sheriff thought. *Those fishermen probably exaggerated her condition. Probably looked worse than it is. Things tend to look different out in the dark woods.*

"You on your way, sheriff?" Long's voice came from the radio.

"Headed your way. Passin' Honey Loaf," Gil answered.

"You need to get here asap. This is the worst thing I've ever seen."

Sensing the urgency in the deputy's voice, the sheriff flipped on his red and blue lights and fired up the siren. As the lawman sped up, he observed flashing lights and heard the siren of an ambulance on the road in front of his squad car. The two emergency vehicles pulled up at the scene simultaneously, the medical personnel bolted from the ambulance, hurriedly pulled a gurney from the back, and guided by Long's motioning, headed toward the victim.

"What's that ungodly smell?" Gil asked as he pulled a handkerchief from his hip pocket and covered his nose and mouth. The stench of burnt flesh mixed with the smell of gasoline drifted through the air and filled his nostrils.

"Worse thing I've ever seen," Long responded. "Whoever attacked the poor girl apparently doused her with gas and set her on fire. Just like the fishermen reported, even her own mother wouldn't know her."

"Good, God, and she's still alive?" Gil questioned. "You weren't exaggeratin'." The tough former soldier thought he had seen everything when he served in Korea. There his buddies' mutilated bodies fell dead right next to him, but the condition of the rape victim made the horrific things he had witnessed in battle pale. The gruesome picture and the horrible smell made the lawman's stomach churn and lurch and the sour taste of vomit filled his mouth as he heaved and puked violently. "Sorry, guys. I thought I could handle most anything, but this. . . this is . . .I got no words. Sorry y'all had to see me puke my guts out."

"No problem, Boss," Long replied. "I did the same thing."

"Was she able to speak, tell you anything?"

"Yeah, she tried to. Said she had been raped, but she did not identify her attacker. All she said was that he lived over there and pointed toward town and that he drove a red Toyota pickup."

"Good, God, a red Toyota pickup?" Gil gasped. "I could have had the bastard in custody."

"What are you talking about?" Long questioned.

"I saw a red Toyota truck in town when I was headed out here. The idiot was drivin' down Harrison Avenue like a madman. Ran right through the red light. If I hadn't been in a hurry to get out here, I woulda pulled him over and hauled him in."

"Did y'all say he was driving a red Toyota?" George asked when he overheard the conversation.

"That's right," Gil answered. "Why?"

"The guy that was supposed to stay with her while we went for help was driving a red Toyota pickup. Had a beat up old white camper shell on the back."

"Good God, that's the same one I saw speeding down Harrison Avenue. Long, you'd best radio dispatch and have 'em put out an APB on that truck."

"Will do, Boss. I'm surprised he didn't finish her off while y'all were gone," Long asserted.

"I don't think he ever found her," Barry injected. "He didn't really listen when we tried to tell him where she was. Just said he knew the spot."

"It doesn't appear that there was a struggle where y'all found her. I bet he went back where ever he raped her thinkin' she was still there," Gil assumed. "What is that wet spot in the dirt next to her?"

"Smells like pee," Long suggested as he leaned down and inspected the spot.

"Probably hers, but you'd better bag some of that dirt," Gil instructed.

The medical personnel choked and gagged as they did what they could for Marcia, but out of pure determination they did not throw up. More skin peeled off Marcia's body as the EMTs gently picked her up and placed her on the gurney. With lights flashing and sirens blaring they raced toward the small hospital in Leadville.

"What's that on the ground?" Gil asked as he surveyed the area in the brush near the road where the fishermen found Marcia.

"Looks like a glove," Long answered. "Maybe it belongs to the rapist."

"Yeah, bag it," Gil replied. "Could be a key piece of evidence."

As deputy Long reached for the "glove", once again the contents of his stomach filled his throat and mouth. The smelly substance burned as it blew out through his nose. "Boss, it ain't a glove. It's...it's...my God, it's the skin off her hand," Long shrieked as he quickly jerked his hand back when he realized what he saw. "Must have slipped off when the paramedics picked her up. I've never seen anything like it, it's all in one piece just like a glove."

"Are you sure that's what it is?" Gil questioned.

"Look for yourself," Long answered as he backed away.

"Good, Lord. I've never seen anything so gruesome," the sheriff responded when he realized that his deputy had identified the object correctly.

* * *

"I've never heard of such a thing," Randy noted. "You mean it was all in one piece like someone had pulled a glove off?"

"Exactly," Gil replied. "The rest of her skin just peeled off in strips, but it came off her hand all intact."

"It was probably a blessing that the poor girl died," Katy asserted as she wiped away a tear. "The scarring on her body would have paled in comparison to that on her soul."

"You are probably right. She didn't deserve...I mean nobody deserves what she had to go through," Gil replied.

* * *

The sun peeked over the horizon through the mountain passes shortly after Gil and the medical personnel arrived on the scene. By the time the EMTs attended to the gravely injured girl and loaded her in the ambulance for transport to the hospital in Leadville, the early morning rays of sunshine illuminated the area. It became obvious to the lawmen that the attack had not taken place in the location where the fishermen discovered Marcia. No sign of a struggle existed in the area, but a trail of blood, mashed-down brush, strips of skin along with pieces of flesh, and drag marks in the dirt indicated that the victim had crawled to the spot.

"Long, set up a road block at the highway and don't let anybody get by it. Radio dispatch and get every available man out here. We need to search everywhere until we find the scene where the bastard attacked her."

How in God's name could she have crawled so far in that condition? Gil thought as he followed the blood, flesh, and drag marks a quarter mile until he arrived at the spot where Herron had parked the Toyota and commenced the attack.

Long rejoined him at the scene after he left another deputy in charge of the road block. "You think this is where it happened?"

"Not much sign of a struggle here either," Gil answered. "You know if she had the guts to drag herself all that way, she woulda fought him like hell."

"Probably so, but there are tire tracks and fresh oil on the ground. Somebody's parked here in the last few hours. Had to be him. Who else would be out here in the middle of the night unless they were up to no good?"

Gil stood at the top of the ravine and looked through his binoculars in every direction and he caught a glimpse of something white at the bottom of the hill. As he and Deputy Long started down the rise they observed more drag marks, pieces of flesh, and strips of skin that formed a trail like the one they followed from up near the road.

"Apparently, she crawled up out of the wash and I spotted something white at the bottom," Gil informed. "Can't be sure, but looks like tennis shoes. Let's get down there and check it out, but be careful where you walk. Don't mess up the blood trail."

As the pair drew close to the bottom of the gulley they spotted a pair of tennis shoes, a red gas can, and a large area of scorched earth. "This must be where he set her on fire," Long speculated.

"Probably is the spot, but, wasn't she naked from the waist down when those guys found her?" Gil questioned.

"Yes, she was," Long answered. "What are you getting at?"

"This is obviously where he doused her with gas and set her on fire, but I don't think the rape took place here."

"Why not?" Long asked.

"She was naked when they found her so where are her clothes? They aren't around here anywhere. You know that violent bastard ripped them off before he raped her."

"Good point, but where?"

As the two lawmen searched for the actual site of the rape they observed more smashed brush, small barefoot tracks that were obviously Marcia's, and much larger foot imprints in the dirt. These telltale signs formed another trail up the other side of the ravine. When the sheriff and his deputy ascended the hill, and arrived at the top they realized that they had located the scene where the violent rape had taken place. There they found Marcia's tan pants and a pair of men's white jockey shorts.

"What, Boss?" Long asked as he observed a puzzled look on Gil's face. "What's bothering you?"

"Her underwear, Long. Where are they? She didn't have them on and they're not here with the other items. Get pictures of everything and then bag the items," Gil instructed. "I want to get back to town and check on the girl. You and the other guys keep on looking and see if you can find her underwear or anything else we can use as evidence."

* * *

"How did y'all figure out who she was?" Randy asked.

"From her father," Gil answered.

"How did you know to contact him?"

"Didn't. He called us."

"Now I'm really confused," Randy declared.

* * *

"Sheriff, Howard Leggett called looking for Marcia again. Said she didn't come home again last night," the dispatcher announced.

Good, God," Gil thought. *Could Marcia be the victim?* "Get back ahold of Howard and have him meet me at the hospital."

"Gil, are you thinking the same thing I am?" the dispatcher asked.

"Yeah, but don't say anything to Howard. We could be wrong."

"One other thing, Boss. There's an old Ford pickup out on the parking lot and I think it is Marcia's."

"Run the plates and get back to me."

A few minutes later the dispatcher reported back with the information that the truck in fact belonged to Howard Leggett. Gil knew then that the poor girl who had been raped and burned was most likely Marcia Leggett.

How in God's name am I going to tell Howard that his girl has been brutally raped and set on fire and is so badly burned that none of us recognized her? How? My God, how?

* * *

"How on earth were you able to tell him?" Randy questioned.

"One of the hardest things I've ever had to do," Gill answered. "But I had to do it."

* * *

"Why did you have me meet you here?" Howard asked anxiously as he and the sheriff arrived at the hospital.

"Do you recognize these?" Gil asked as he removed the tan pants and white tennis shoes from the evidence bags.

"They are Marcia's," he answered. "She was wearing 'em when she left the house last night to go meet her friend Linda at the courthouse parking lot. Why have you got 'em?"

"So, she was supposed to meet Linda?"

"Yeah, Linda Elliott. You know, the Elliott family that lives near the old Oro City site south of town."

"Yeah, I know the family, but . . ." Gil stopped talking momentarily, reached deep inside himself, and mustered up the courage and told the father what had happened.

"Howard, I just don't know how to tell you, so I'll just spit it out. Marcia was apparently abducted and raped sometime during the night."

"Oh, my God. I begged her not to go. Told her something just didn't feel right. Is she okay?"

"I haven't told you . . . haven't told you the worst part yet," Gil informed haltingly.

"What could be worse?" Howard questioned as tears welled up in his eyes.

"This is hard."

"Oh, God, Gil, don't tell me she's dead."

"No, she's not dead, but damn close to it. I hate to have to tell you, but whoever raped her beat her to a pulp and then doused her with gasoline and set her on fire. She's got severe burns over at least seventy-five percent of her body, her skull is fractured, kinda smashed in. Apparently, he hit her with a tire iron or something, and her lungs are all messed up from inhaling the smoke and flames."

"OH, GOD, NO!" Howard shrieked. "Why . . .why would anybody do such a thing? My God, he done got what he was after when he raped her. Why didn't he just leave her be?"

"Probably afraid she could identify him, so he tried to kill her."

"How did y'all find her?"

"A couple of fishermen found her out by Turquoise Lake. They did what they could for her and came to town and alerted us. If they hadn't found her she'd 'a died out there."

"I want to see her," Howard requested.

"Okay, Howard, but prepare yourself. She's not recognizable."

As Gil and Howard approached the room where the injured girl lay unconscious, the father observed a deputy that stood by the door. "Why a deputy at the door?" he asked.

"It's a long story, but the bastard apparently went back and tried to find her probably to. . .to finish the job," Gil answered hesitantly. "We just figured we should keep her guarded just in case."

"My God, Gil, do you think he'll come back?"

"Probably not, but we're not takin' any chances."

Overcome with emotion, Howard broke down and sobbed mournfully as he slumped into a chair that stood next to his precious daughter's bed. Covered in bandages, his baby girl, the apple of his eye, lay unresponsive as the father expressed his undying love. "My God, baby, what did that monster do to you?" he questioned between sobs.

"Howard, they're going to take her to the University of Colorado Anschutz Burn Center by helicopter," Gil informed as he entered the room. They've done all they can for her here and if she stands any chance of surviving they've got to get her to the burn center."

"I want to go with her," Howard implored.

"They won't let you go in the 'copter and you're in no shape to drive that far. One of my deputies will take you in a squad car. They'll get you there as fast as they can."

"Sheriff, they've found the Toyota," the dispatcher voice announced excitedly.

"Where?"

"Up near Copper Mountain. Ran off the side of highway twenty-four. The truck's a couple a hundred feet down the side of the mountain."

"Any sign of the driver?" Gil questioned.

"Not so far, but the mountain rescuers are going down to the truck as we speak."

"Chances are he's dead," the sheriff assumed. "That don't hurt my feelin's, but I would like to have done him in myself."

"That doesn't sound like you, Sheriff," the dispatcher replied.

"You didn't see what he did to Marcia. I'm headin' out to Copper Mountain to see for myself."

Just as Gil arrived at the crash site the rescue team had returned from their mission at the bottom of the deep ravine. They had not located Herron in or anywhere near the red Toyota pickup. Highly disappointed, Gil realized that the murdering rapist apparently had escaped capture for the time being.

"Did y'all find anything in the pickup?"

"Just these," one of the rescuers answered as he held up a pair of white panties and a blurry Polaroid picture of a girl engulfed in flames.

"Good, God! The sick bastard probably took them as a trophy. The sick son-of-a-bitch took pictures. What the hell kinda monster does that? Did y'all get the plate numbers?"

"Plates were missing," they replied. "Probably removed 'em to avoid being identified."

Highly disappointed that the identifying objects had been removed, Gil declared that whoever the perpetrator was, he had a date with destiny no matter how long the search and apprehension took.

I will not rest until I catch the bastard and see him getting the needle, Gil thought as he drove back to Leadville.

* * *

"What a horrible day that must have been for you and everybody else, Gil," Randy asserted.

"It was that," Gil replied. "First time I'd ever seen my deputies cry and damn near ever one of 'em that was out at the scene puked their guts out."

"Sounds awful."

"Boy, you cannot imagine. She was Howard Leggett's baby girl, a real flesh and blood person. With all that we had seen, it got worse."

"How in God's name could it have gotten any worse?"

* * *

Gil had intended a visit with Linda Elliot that evening, but the situation deteriorated drastically as the sun slowly disappeared behind the mountains when he headed back to Leadville from the crash site. The current turn of events upset the sheriff and he postponed the interview until the next morning.

"I've got bad news," the dispatcher announced over the radio.

"Couldn't be as bad as this day has been so far," Gil responded.

"Oh, yes it can. I just don't have the heart to say it."

"Spit it out," the sheriff instructed.

"Just got a call from the burn center. . ."

"And?"

"Marcia Leggett succumbed to her injuries a short while ago. We are now looking for a murderer."

"Did Howard get there before she died?"

"Barely. He'd only been there about five minutes."

"At least he got there. I'm glad he did."

Gil pulled the squad car off the road, sat in silence for a long time, and he cried.

CHAPTER 7

THE HOMECOMING

"THAT WAS A HORRIBLE NIGHT," GIL EXCLAIMED. "I JUST TOSSED and turned the whole night. I didn't sleep a wink. My heart ached for Marcia and her family, my mind wondered how anyone could be so evil, and my soul cried out to God. 'Why? Why God, why?' Marcia's horribly mutilated and burned body, that glove of skin, the strips of skin and chunks of flesh that we found along the blood trail, the scorched earth where he set her on fire, and everything that I saw at the crime scene, the excruciating torture, mutilation, and pain she suffered, and finally her death all kept running amuck in my mind. The white jockey shorts that we found made it clear what his perverted intentions were and testified to what he had done. I wondered who had worn the jockey shorts, and what kind of a monster we were dealing with. I wanted to get my hands on whoever it was and tear him apart limb by limb. If I coulda got my hands on him I think I would'a beat the sorry bastard to death."

"Settle down, Gil," Katy admonished. "Don't get yourself all riled, your blood pressure'll go up and make you stroke out. It's over with now."

"I know," Gil responded. "But it still burns deep down in my soul whenever I think about that poor girl, what she suffered, and what her family will live with for the rest of their lives."

"I've got no way of knowing exactly how you feel," Randy responded. "But, I imagine if I had been so closely connected with the case like y'all are I would have wanted to kill the son-of-bitch."

"Now look what you've done, Gil. You've got Randy to talking like that," Katy scolded.

"The next few days were a real sorrowful time in Leadville," Gil informed. "From the gold and silver mining days until today, this has always been a lively, even rowdy, and boisterous town, but the events of that night quietened everybody down. People moved about solemnly and spoke in hushed tones if at all. Everyone in town mourned for Marcia and her family. They wanted the inconceivably evil bastard caught and justice done. I think if we had taken him into custody in the first couple of weeks I would have had a real big problem on my hands."

"How so?" Randy questioned.

"Everybody was so riled up I think they woulda tried to lynch him, and I don't know if I coulda stopped it. I'm not even sure I woulda wanted to stop it, but it was my job and I guess I woulda tried," Gil answered.

"Yes, and you mighta got yourself killed in the process," Katy added. "Folks were just that upset."

"Not only were they riled up, but they also lived with the fear that the monster might still be around and would strike again. For some time, you didn't see a girl or a woman alone anywhere in town. They were either in groups or accompanied by a man, and you can bet just about ever' man and a lot of women were packin' heat."

"A lot of us gals just holed up and only left the house when we absolutely had to," Katy added. "I had myself a .22 pistol and I woulda used it if any creep matching the description had come anywhere close to me."

"I imagine everyone felt just like that," Randy asserted.

"Yes, they did."

"That's not a good way to live," Randy added.

"I don't know for sure but what I mighta pulled off my badge and joined the mob for a lynching. But regardless of the fear and anger and like it or not, I still had a job to do," Gil grimaced.

* * *

This is gonna be another real difficult job, Gil thought as he headed south toward the Elliott home. Morning rays of sunshine peeked through the mountains in the east and cast a golden glow over the normally happy-go-lucky hamlet of Leadville. The quaint, sleepy little town nestled high in the Rocky Mountains had a main street lined with historic nineteenth-century buildings. The Heritage Museum, housed in the old Carnegie Library, stood at one end of Harrison Avenue and the famous old Silver Dollar Saloon occupied a space near the southern edge of the main drag. The place appeared as a peaceful, safe haven from the violent world beyond the mountains, but the ungodly events of that night changed everything. The high valley seemed anything but peaceful to Sheriff Gentry.

Gil knew that delivery of his grim message to the Elliott family would destroy any small sense of wellbeing they possessed. *It's kinda early, but I want to tell Linda what happened before she hears it through the grapevine, if she hasn't already. Bad news travels fast in a little town like Leadville.*

"OH, MY GOD, NO! NOT MARCIA" Linda screamed. "It can't be true. Please tell me it isn't true. She's my best friend. She can't be . . . be dead."

"I'm sorry, Linda, I wish I could say it's not so, but it is true," Gil declared. "I got no words to make it any easier."

"I knew that sorry devil was up to no good. Tried to lure us into his trailer. Offered us whiskey and a joint," Linda declared between sobs after Gil informed her of the previous night's events.

"Who are you talkin' about?" the sheriff questioned.

"I didn't like it when he started talking about us looking sexy in the moonlight, and how we could get all relaxed and comfortable and have a good time. I heard him say under his breath that he'd give us something we'd never forget. Kinda like he was thinking out loud. I figured I knew what he meant by a good time and what that unforgettable something was. I wanted no part of it and neither did Marcia, but she did like to tease. I knew he was up to no good, but I never expected anything so horrible. Oh, my God, not Marcia," Linda sobbed.

"Who, Linda? Who?"

"Richard Herron."

"I don't recall that name," Gil noted. "Is he one of the boys from school? I thought I knew 'em all."

"No, he's an older guy, probably twenty-four or twenty-five. Works out at the Climax."

"Where does Herron live?" the sheriff quizzed.

"In an old trailer at the back of Honey Loaf Campground."

"I won't bother you no more right now, but after the shock kinda wears off you need to come down to the office and give a full statement of everything that happened last night. I know it'll be hard, but it's real important that we get as much information about him as we can. We've got to catch 'im and get 'im off the streets before he hurts somebody else. Sometime in the next few hours, whenever you feel up to it. The sooner the better," the lawman instructed.

"Oh, God, I feel so guilty. I shoulda insisted that Marcia come with me when he let me out of his truck at the courthouse. If she had, she'd still be alive. It's all my fault," Linda lamented. "You've got to catch that monster real quick and I hope what I got to report helps."

Gil heard Linda's sobs and cries as they wafted through the early morning mountain air when he returned to his patrol car. The guilt that Linda felt tore at the sheriff's heartstrings. He knew that she bore no responsibility for the horrific end to Marcia's life, but he also realized that she most likely felt a pang of culpability that would last a lifetime. Richard Herron had not only raped and murdered Howard Leggett's baby girl, but he had also placed an undeserved blight on the life of Linda Elliott. A single tear trickled down the caring sheriff's ruddy masculine face.

"How long you gonna be, Sheriff?" the dispatcher questioned.

"I'm on my way back to the office now," Gil answered.

"Good. You need to get here quick as you can. Howard and Esther Leggett are in your office waiting for you. Boss, they are just sitting there in total silence. They're not talking to each other and she just keeps glaring at him. It's plumb unsettling and I just don't know what to say to 'em."

"Nothin' you can say. Just take 'em a cup of coffee and let 'em know I'm on my way."

"Who done this to our baby girl?" Howard asked as Gil entered his office and sat behind the desk across from the grieving parents.

"We know who did it," Gil answered. "A guy by the name of Richard Herron lured Marcia and her friend, Linda, out to his old trailer at Honey Loaf Campground under the pretense of hirin' 'em to clean the place. Me and Deputy Long'll be headed out there after awhile, soon as the judge signs a search warrant."

"What about Linda?" Howard inquired. "Did she get away? Is she all right?"

"She smelled a rat and insisted that he bring her back to town," Gil answered. "She doesn't know if Marcia went back with him willingly or if he forced her."

"She was just too trusting. Something she learned from you, Howard Leggett. It's all your fault. Just like her father, she never saw a stranger and trusted everybody," Esther declared as she glared at her husband.

Gil sensed that not only had the murderer destroyed their lives, but he had put a heavy strain on the Leggett marriage. It seemed to the sheriff that in her need to place blame, Esther had projected that responsibility onto her husband. The ever-patient Howard did not return the assessment of guilt to his wife. He spoke to her lovingly as he took her hand in his, "Now, Esther, calm yourself. You don't mean that. You're just upset."

"Sheriff, you caught 'im yet?" Esther questioned as she jerked her hand away from her compassionate husband.

"No, ma'am. Not yet, but we will," the sheriff promised. "I promise you I will not rest until he's caught and gets the death penalty."

"What about Marcia?" Howard sobbed. "We left her at the burn center. When can we bring her home?"

"The Medical Examiner from Denver will pick her up this morning and take her for an autopsy."

"Don't want no autopsy," Howard cried. "Won't have nobody cuttin' her up."

"I'm sorry, Howard, but that's the way it works in a case like this. Got no choice. It's the law. Soon as they're done, the guys from Hailey-Fenton Funeral home will go get her and bring her home."

* * *

"Doesn't seem fair to me that Esther blamed Howard," Randy noted.

"Me either," Gil replied. "But, she did, and their relationship was never the same. Folks say it was already tenuous at best, but what happened to their daughter totally destroyed it."

"Did they get a divorce?"

"No. They stayed together until Howard died, but it was no longer a 'marriage.'"

"What did you find at Herron's trailer?" Randy inquired.

"You name it and we found it," Gil replied.

"What do you mean?"

"Real disgustin' and disturbin' stuff."

* * *

Armed with a search warrant, Gil and Deputy Long entered the shabby, rusted-out old trailer where Herron had lived. Polaroid pictures of Marcia and Linda taken from a distance at school and other places around Leadville disturbed the lawmen as much as the piles of disgusting pornographic magazines and photos that they found.

"Did you ever see anything so gross?" Deputy Long asked as he placed stacks of publications in an evidence box—magazines that showed repulsive acts in explicit photographs, many of which involved teenagers and young kids.

"I thought I'd seen ever'thing when I was in the Army, but I never saw anything like some of this stuff. I'm supposed to know the law," Gil responded. "And a lot of this stuff is illegal, particularly the magazines with pictures of teenagers and young kids."

"These pictures of Marcia and Linda kinda make you think he had a plan," Long declared. "Really bothers me that there are pictures of Linda."

"Yeah, me too," Gil responded. "Kinda like he had plans for both girls. Soon as we get back to town, you need to get out to Elliott's place and tell them to be real cautious. Insist that they do not let Linda ever be alone. You never know, a crazy nut job like

Herron might come back."

"Maybe we should patrol the area near their house real regular," Long suggested.

"Good idea, better safe than sorry," Gil responded.

With heads bowed and tears that flowed like the many streams around Leadville, as a show of support dozens of folks lined Harrison Avenue when the hearse from Hailey-Fenton Funeral Home returned Marcia to the town she loved. She had come home for the last time. Businesses all over the town displayed wreaths, closed their doors, and a large contingent of townspeople battled the elements as they lined up and paid their respects. Gil had never before witnessed such a show of solidarity in the mountain village.

Snow showers and stiff cold north winds rolled through the high mountain valley and filled the air as the entire town of Leadville shut down on the frigid October morning. Most of the citizens of Leadville gathered at the First Baptist Church on Mountain View Drive where they said goodbye to Marcia Leggett. Undeterred by the freezing temperature and icy precipitation, many who attended stood in the church yard since the sanctuary overflowed with humanity. Floral arrangements of every description, red roses, yellow roses, carnations, forget-me-nots, and lilies graced the altar. Many sniffles, sobs, and cries echoed through the church as evidence that the tragedy had an unbelievably huge negative affect on the populous.

The townspeople rallied around the Leggett family and supported them with love during the sorrowful time. They showed their genuine concern with donations that covered the funeral expenses. The caring folks realized that the badly burned remains necessitated a closed casket, so they purchased a beautiful gleaming copper coffin with an elegantly appointed exterior as an expression of love and affection for Marcia and her grieving family.

Many mourners accompanied Marcia and her family to the Evergreen Cemetery on the northwest edge of town. A lone aspen tree that had retained its golden leaves when others in the grove above the cemetery stood bare reminded Gil of the golden streets of heaven where Marcia Leggett now walked. When the brilliant yellow leaves fluttered in the cold winds, the sheriff knew without a doubt that Marcia had said farewell as she embarked on her journey to the other side. A knowing gleam appeared in Howard's eyes when he glanced at the "quakies" as their leaves slowly drifted to the ground. The father knew that his daughter had said goodbye and had moved on from this earth to her heavenly home. It gave him a measure of comfort, but still he grieved.

Esther Leggett sat silent and stoic as the look of unbearable grief showed on her face. Howard laid his arms, hands, and head on the casket and moaned sorrowfully as the pastor concluded the graveside service and folks departed. How could his life continue with the image that now filled his soul, the image of his baby girl tortured, raped, and burned beyond recognition?

* * *

"I just don't know how he stood it," Randy declared.

"Me either," Katy added. "It was horrible just being on the jury and seeing and hearing all the horrific details, but to have it happen to your own daughter. Unbearable!"

"What nobody at the cemetery knew was that they were being watched by none other than the perpetrator," Gil informed. "Richard Herron had returned. He watched, gloated, and reveled at what he had done. The thoughts he had of the ungodly act excited and aroused the rapist and we later found several aspen leaves with a sticky residue on 'em at the site from where the monster had observed the burial. It turned out to be Herron's semen."

"You mean he...?" Randy asked.

"Yeah, even as they lowered her in the ground," Gil answered.

"I never have heard of anything so sick. I cannot even imagine such a thing."

* * *

The bitch shoulda gave me what I wanted, willingly, the highly excited Herron thought as he crouched behind a large boulder and watched the interment. *She'd still be alive and we coulda had a lot more good times, but the struggle did make it more exciting. Oh, well, there's always that Linda girl.* The murdering rapist had returned.

The deranged maniac's familiarity with Leadville and the surrounding mountains helped him evade arrest for nearly a year, but Sheriff Gentry never gave up. The legendary lawman enjoyed a magnificent reputation as one who did not rest until he caught his man. Gil received numerous reports that Herron had been sighted in the area and the sheriff checked out each lead.

Herron positioned himself out of sight on a ridge high above the Elliott home, he watched the family as they came and went, observed the regularity of patrol cars, and learned the pattern of both. The criminal observed the father as he instructed the daughter in the use of a handgun and he figured that she, like most folks in Leadville, did not venture out unarmed. The stalker realized that Linda's family and the sheriff's department diligently guarded his prey and thwarted any attempt at fulfillment of his perverted plan.

I'll catch her by herself sometime and then 'let the fun begin', he thought as he disappeared into the mountains.

* * *

"So he did come back to town. Did he ever make a move on Linda Elliott?" the nephew questioned.

"Not for several months," Gil answered. "He hid up in the mountains 'til spring. First at old Vicksburg and the ghost town of Winfield, and finally way off up in the mountains someplace. The unattended walkin' tour museum area of Vicksburg frequented in the summer by tourists, shut down durin' the winter months and Herron knew none of the folks that had cabins up there would use 'em as long as the frigid weather persisted, so he had free rein of the place for a spell."

"What did he plan on doing for food?" Randy asked.

"A lot of the people with vacation or weekend cabins up there kept them stocked with supplies, and Herron was an avid hunter so he figured he was all set to ride out the cold season," Gil answered. "When I got wind that he might be in that area, the chase began."

CHAPTER 8

THE CHASE

"HOW DID YOU GET WIND THAT HERRON MIGHT BE AT VICKSBURG?" Randy asked.

"I realized that he knew the area like the back of his hand. While investigatin' his back-ground I found out that he had spent numerous summers in Colorado. Herron and his father visited the area many times, camping out in wilderness areas. Richard Sr. taught Jr. survival skills, and most likely on these outings the unconventional father probably introduced his son to deviant stuff. Never could prove it, but most folks figured that the father initiated incestuous activities with the son. They didn't stay very close to town, but camped out in the backwoods around Leadville and other places like Aspen, Vail, Breckenridge, Buena Vista, and sometimes real far off the grid in some mountain cabin."

"Sounds like he kinda had an unfair advantage, knowing the area so well," Randy responded.

"Yeah, he sorta did. Few people really knew the loner, he didn't have much to do with anybody except young women, but those who did know him, told us that he hated the area of California where he lived. He liked the solitude of the Rocky Mountains and he loved the outdoors. After he got a little older he spent as much of his spare time as he could in the mountains, summer and winter without his father. They said he bragged that he never wore clothes in the summer, just ran around through the mountains in his birthday suit. The nut job told 'em that runnin' around naked made him feel free."

"What kinda crazy person does that?" Randy questioned.

"A perverted lunatic, that's who," Gil answered. "They also reported that he even slept out in the snow many nights, was well acclimated to winter conditions, and knew how to survive. For some unknown reason the recluse had a special attachment to area ghost towns."

"Yeah, but from what I've read and what you've told me there are a bunch of old ghost towns scattered throughout the mountains," Randy noted. "You called him a loner so maybe he liked the invisible residents better than flesh and blood people."

"That's probably right, and they probably tolerated him 'cause he couldn't harm 'em like he could real people," Gil responded. "From what I found out he had few, if any, real friends. Had little to do with other men and had an unhealthy fixation on females, especially teenaged girls. The women who worked at the Climax told me that he 'creeped' them out. Old Vicksburg, Winfield, and the Leadville mining district were apparently his favorite haunts."

* * *

Gil realized that the vast mountainous region around Leadville presented an almost impossible search area, especially in winter. Heavy snows, ice, and temperatures well below zero normally moved into the region by late September or early October each year, and 1979 was no exception. After an unseasonably warm September an arctic front descended on Leadville and the surrounding countryside on the last day of the month. The sheriff knew that if he did not catch Herron before subzero weather completely engulfed Lake County, the manhunt operations would grind to a halt until spring thaws brought more suitable conditions.

"Sheriff, pick up the phone," Deputy Long instructed. "I think you will find this of interest."

"Sheriff Gentry here," he answered.

"This is Nick over at Colorado Mountain Rescue,"

"Hey, Nick. Haven't heard from you in a while. You got somethin' for me?"

"Yeah, Gil. I just got back from a routine training flight over your area and I saw smoke coming from one of the cabins up at Vicksburg. Damn unusual for this time of year. Those weekenders don't normally go up there in the snow. I circled back at a lower altitude for a second look just to be sure. There was smoke, all right. Thought you might find this interesting since I know you've got a fugitive on the run somewhere in these mountains."

"You bet it is," Gil responded. "I appreciate you keepin' an eye on things. I'll be headed up that way shortly."

"Better take a four-wheel drive. That crooked road is pretty darn narrow and dangerous in good weather. Quite a bit of snow up there already. You be careful."

"Will do, Nick," Gil replied. "I gotta take the risk. We need to catch that sorrow devil before he hurts someone else."

"I hear you," Nick responded.

Damn it, Herron thought when he heard the helicopter that flew over Vicksburg. *Gotta be mountain rescue. Nobody else'd be flying up here in this weather. Probably looking for some crazy hiker lost in the snow. Probably didn't notice the smoke.*

The fugitive had built a roaring fire that burned brightly in the native stone fireplace. The heat filled the cabin, and the man relaxed all snug and warm, stretched out in a lounge chair with the thought that no one ever ventured out to the remote area in winter. The large fire produced a vast amount of smoke, and brisk winds carried its billows high in the atmosphere. On his second flyover of the area at a lower altitude, Nick detected the smell of a wood fire and he knew that someone occupied the cabin whence the vapors ascended.

That's real odd, Nick thought. *Nobody ever comes up here this time of year. Roads are darn near impassable with all the snow and ice. Anybody in their right mind wouldn't venture up this far in this weather. Wonder if it could be that raping murderer ever body's looking for? I best let the sheriff know.*

Several minutes passed and the sound of the aircraft seemed further in the distance to Herron. He relaxed with the false assurance that danger had passed, and he opened a pornographic magazine to a real explicit photo. *First time I catch her by herself, I'm gonna have me a go at that Linda girl,* he thought as he stared hypnotically at a photo of his current conquest that he kept tucked inside the publication filled with lewd pictures.

Whap, whap, whap, the deafening sound of spinning rotors on the low-flying helicopter jolted the aroused pervert out of his fantasy and back to reality. He dropped the magazine, ran across the cabin, and peered out the window. *It's mountain rescue, all right, came back for a second look and now they know somebody's here. Damn it! I was all set for the winter and now I've gotta move on. I know damn well they'll report to Sheriff Gentry and that persistent cuss'll most likely come looking for me.*

The fugitive wanted as much time and space between himself and the sheriff as possible, so he hurriedly stuffed his belongings in his backpack. The desperado ransacked the cabin in search of edible items. He located numerous cans filled with vegetables, soups, and meat. The desperado picked up several containers of Spam, along with other packaged nonperishable foods and placed as many as possible into the rucksack.

That oughta hold me for a while. I can kill some game. Got a goodly amount of dope. Got it made. Just gotta get out of here real quick before that sheriff shows up. Don't know why he's gotta be so damn persistent. After all, I just gave that bitch what she had coming. the depraved excuse of a man thought.

* * *

"He really thought Marcia had it coming?" Randy questioned.

"I think so," Gil answered. "That's the way his warped mind worked. He thought she shoulda just gave in to his demands."

"Do you think that would have saved her?"

"Maybe, but probably not," Gil replied. "I think the crazy S-O-B woulda killed her regardless. I believe the sick bastard got off as much from the torturin' and killin' as he did from the rape."

"Good grief. What a sorry excuse for a human being," Randy declared.

* * *

The desperate outlaw removed several bottles of Jack Daniels from inside a cabinet where he found them, and in his haste, he knocked one to the floor. Shards of glass from the broken bottle and splashes of whiskey scattered across the room when it landed with a crash. *Damn! What a waste of good whiskey. Better take the rest with me,* he thought. *May be a while before I come across any more.* The whiskey containers and food items crowded the pack. Herron figured he had just about all he could handle, but he figured he had everything he needed.

The devious conniver placed several more logs on the fire until it flared up and filled the fireplace to capacity. *That'll throw 'em off,* he thought. *With a big fire still burning they'll think I've just left and they'll look for me close by, and meanwhile I'll be well on my way to Winfield.*

The outlaw glanced around the cabin one last time and made sure he had not left any identifying item behind before he headed out. He did not realize that the porno magazine and Linda's picture still lay on the floor, a dead giveaway to his identity.

More heavy snow showers descended on the area as Herron exited the cabin and started the long hike up the mountain toward Winfield, one of his favorite ghost towns. The renegade considered the abundant white icy precipitation a good thing since it covered his tracks and left no trail for anyone who pursued him. Herron knew the mountainous area well, understood the severity of the weather, and dressed accordingly with items he had retrieved from his trailer and stuffed in his large backpack. He had stopped there and gathered his belongings on his way to the Climax mine after he committed the rape and murder.

The criminal had told George and Barry that he was headed to work when in fact he only stopped at the mine long enough to draw his pay. Then he disposed of the red Toyota and headed to Vicksburg on foot. Even though the hike took several hours, an unusually warm September day made the hike a pleasant experience as the pervert reveled in thoughts of what he had done, thoughts that excited and aroused him. He avoided Leadville on his journey for fear of apprehension. Herron skirted the town and made his way by back roads protected from view by the wilderness of timber, boulders, and mountains. Upon his arrival at the ghost town he assumed that he had landed at his home for the winter. The complacent man had not considered discovery by Rocky Mountain Rescue.

The deranged maniac had discovered a radio in the cabin where he had taken refuge. He stayed informed of events in Leadville and Lake County as he listened intently to local newscast. *I've got to be there*, he thought when the announcer told of funeral plans for

Herron's victim. *I'll hike down the mountain the day before, camp out in the woods, watch 'em put the bitch in the ground and then head back up here.*

Herron deemed the cold blast that covered the mountains with snow and ice a good thing since as long as the wintery mix fell from the heavens his tracks disappeared. As the murdering rapist prepared for the trek to Winfield, he donned heavy socks, calf-high boots, long johns, several pair of pants with their legs stuffed down inside the boots, and three flannel shirts. A fur-lined cap with ear muffs, and a woolen scarf that covered his face and a heavy coat completed the preparations. The renegade wore most of the clothing in his possession and left ample room in his backpack for food and whiskey. Herron knew that the normal two-hour hike up the mountain extended to three or four under current conditions, so he prepared himself well. The thick layers of clothing protected the hiker as he braved the frigid temperatures and trudged through the deep snow toward his refuge in Winfield.

Gil's eagle eyes combed the countryside for signs of the fugitive as the four-wheel drive Toyota Land Cruiser chugged slowly up the crooked slick mountain road. The sheriff figured the desperado was still hold up in one of the cabins when he spotted smoke as he drew close to Vicksburg. The lawman parked the vehicle a quarter mile down the road from the ghost town. He quietly hiked the distance, maintaining the element of surprise, or so he thought. The sheriff approached the cabin where the smoke billowed with gun in hand, cocked, and ready.

Crouched behind a large boulder Gill issued a demand. "Come out of the cabin with your hands high in the air where I can see 'em."

No response came forth from within the structure, so he

repeated the command. "Come out with your hands up! Still no response.

The sheriff carefully worked his way closer to the building. He dashed from behind the big boulder to another and another until he stood at a vantage point with the front of the cabin in full few. The door stood ajar and Gil saw that no one occupied the house. The fugitive had escaped. The lawman replaced his gun in the holster and proceeded inside where he observed the fire that still burned brightly.

Funny the fire is so big, just like he just left, and from the looks of things he did leave in a hurry, Gil thought as he kicked pieces of the broken whiskey bottle aside. *But there weren't no tracks outside. Been gone long enough that the snow done covered 'em. I'll bet the crafty S-O-B built the fire up to try and throw me off. Gotta get up pretty early in the morning to outfox a fox.*

The sheriff knew he had followed a good lead when he spotted the porno magazine and Linda's picture that still lay on the floor where Herron had dropped them. *Yep, Herron's been here, all right. Really worries me that he kept a picture of Linda with 'im. I know damn well he's got something in mind with her and I can imagine what. I figure he's headed up to Winfield. Several weekend cabins up there and he probably knows it.*

Gil had barely navigated the land cruiser up the crooked slick treacherous road to Vicksburg and the danger of the lane from there to Winfield increased with each curve. He considered his options and formulated a plan. *I'll wait 'til tomorrow and come back with my horse. I'll pull the trailer as far as I can up the road and then Hammer'll take me the rest of the way.*

* * *

"Hammer, that's a funny name for a horse," Randy proclaimed.

"Shows what you know," Gil retorted. "A gun has a trigger and a hammer, right?"

"What's that go to do with anything?" the nephew asked.

"The horse I had back home in my younger days was Trigger, so what else would I call my next one but Hammer?"

"I reckon I've been hanging around you too long," Randy declared. "Believe it or not, that makes sense to me. You gonna call your next one Barrel?"

"Now that would be a stupid name for a horse," Gil replied with a chuckle. "Besides, there probably won't ever be another one. I'm a hair bit too old for that tomfoolery."

"Did you catch him at Winfield?" Randy questioned.

"I was close behind him, but he stayed one step ahead of me like he knew I was comin' for 'im," Gil answered.

* * *

Herron located a suitable cabin when he arrived at the old ghost town of Winfield and entered the structure through an unlocked door. Folks still maintained an element of trust in the 1970s, especially out in the mountainous wilderness. They left cabins unlocked for anyone who passed by and needed shelter or a place to sleep. The wet, cold, and exhausted hiker warmed himself by a fire he laid in the wood stove that stood in one corner of the room. After the fugitive shucked off several layers of clothing, he retrieved some "reading material" from his backpack, and relaxed. Stricken by panic when he realized that he left one of his magazines and a picture of Linda behind in the cabin at Vicksburg, he changed his plan.

Sheriff Gentry ain't no dummy. Soon as he sees that picture he'll figure out that I was there, and he'll know where I'm headed. It's already gettin' dark and I don't reckon he'll come for me 'til tomorrow. I'll get myself a good rest, get up real early, and head up to that old cabin that I know about way up in the mountains. It'll be quite a hike up there, but I know the way. Smart as he is, Gentry probably don't know about the place. He can't drive to it nohow, and there ain't no way even a horse could even get there in this weather. I'll be good there long as my food and whiskey holds out, and seems like I remember the last time I was there, there's several jugs of moonshine stashed in the cabin. What else could a man ask for? Got shelter, food, whiskey, 'shine, and good 'reading' material to keep me entertained. Only thing could make it better, having that Linda girl there to pleasure me. Oh, if only she was here. That sweet thing would be the icing on the cake.

Gentry navigated the land cruiser with the horse trailer behind as far as possible up the steep crooked slick mountain road. At that point he parked the vehicle, led Hammer out of the trailer, mounted the steed, and headed up the mountain toward Winfield. The treacherous journey took several hours and numerous times the half-frozen lawman had thoughts of giving up the chase for the time being. Images of Marcia's mutilated body remained vivid in his mind, so he trudged on, cold and miserable.

Gil surveyed Winfield from a vantage point on the side of a mountain that overlooked the ghost town nestled in a high valley far from civilization. When he scanned the area, the sheriff observed no smoke from any chimney, nor did he see any sign of movement as he scoured the landscape through binoculars. Hammer carried the lawman down the path into the old town where he inspected each building. He found nothing except one more ungodly Polaroid of Marcia. *Seems to me he's leaving stuff just to taunt me,* Gil thought as he retrieved the picture and placed it in an evidence bag. The sheriff decided that Herron had eluded capture on that day, but the persistent lawman did not give up. There would be other days.

* * *

"The chase had ended for the time being. It was impossible to pursue him up in the mountains with all the ice and snow. Just impossible."

"That just don't sound right," Randy declared. "I know you, Uncle Gil. You could track a flea in the dark."

"Yeah, a flea in the dark maybe, but the unrelenting snow covered his tracks. Problem was, I had no idea which direction he had headed, and I couldn't find any signs," Gil informed regretfully. "Sometimes you just gotta know when to back off and regroup."

"You mean you just dropped it?" Randy questioned. "That doesn't sound like the relentless pursuer of justice that I know."

"Hell, no, numb nuts. I didn't just drop it. I said you just have to back off and regroup," Gil snapped.

"Sorry, Gil. Didn't mean no offense. I knew you'd be after him sooner or later."

"Didn't mean to bite your head off, Randy, but thinkin' about this whole business just puts me on edge."

"Yeah, that and the late hour," Katy injected. "Don't you think we should turn in and finish this later?"

"No, darlin'. I want to get the story told, then maybe I can relax. You still with me, Randy?"

"Sure thing, Uncle Gil. I'm anxious to hear the rest of the story."

"Nick and his crew combed the mountains routinely all winter, hoping they'd spot smoke or some other sign of life, but they never spotted a thing. Didn't want to, but I kinda figured we'd find him froze to death in the spring. I wanted him alive, so I could see 'em stick the needle to 'im, or maybe shoot him dead myself if he resisted arrest."

"That sounds real vindictive," Randy asserted.

"Hell, boy, you ain't been listenin' real close. Didn't you hear me tell you what he did to that poor girl?"

"Oh, yeah, I heard, and I think I understand your feelings."

"I sure as hell hope so. You gotta really get into the story and feel it. When you write it you gotta feel it. If you don't, your readers won't either."

CHAPTER 9

THE RETURN

THE LONG GRAY DAYS DRAGGED BY AS THE WINTER OF 1979-1980 passed slowly for Sheriff Gentry and those who lived in the high mountain town of Leadville. Days spent at his desk typing reports on his old Remington typewriter, or time out on routine patrol around Lake County seemed less than productive to Gil so long as Richard Herron remained a free man. The impatient sheriff cleaned his Smith and Wesson Model 629 and loaded it with six rounds of Remington .44 magnum bullets. He knew his firearm of choice provided protection from bear, other animals, or the two-legged varmint that he sought.

The lawman longed for the chase, arrest, trial, and hopefully the execution of the murdering rapist. Old Man Winter did not cooperate as he held on and did not completely relinquish his hold on the mountains until May of 1980. Eight months had passed since the night Herron had raped, tortured and murdered Marcia Leggett. Gil knew that each day without capture gave the rapist an advantage. The lawman doubted that the scoundrel remained close by. He figured the miscreant had moved on to someplace where no one knew him, but unbeknownst to Gil, the criminal still hid in the vicinity.

The sheriff had followed up on numerous tips over the past months, most had been erroneous or had ended when heavy snow, ice, subfreezing temperatures, and impassable roads prevented further exploration. The dedicated, persistent, and downright hardheaded lawman never gave up. Gil relentlessly pursued each lead as his DNA had no markers that indicated a propensity for defeat.

So long as I draw breath I will pursue that murdering rapist to the ends of the earth. I will not go to my grave so long as that bastard still lives, Gil thought as he studied files of the case. *I will not quit until I see them stick the needle to 'im.*

Investigation into Herron's past conducted by law enforcement revealed the nature of his twisted attitude, deranged personality, and perverted mind. As most teenaged males did, Herron enjoyed and felt excitement at what he saw in "girly" magazines. At an early age his interest advanced to hardcore pornographic publications shared with him by his unconventional father. The young Herron experienced repeated arousal while he spent hours watching blurry XXX stag films over and over—movies left in open sight by his father. The teenager developed much more than the normal curiosity about the opposite sex shared by most boys his age. He became obsessive on the subject, and Gil learned that once Herron fixated on a particular girl, he pursued that object of his obsession relentlessly for months. The chase ended only when he fulfilled his desires, or when some other girl attracted his attention.

Herron normally wore tight jeans and form-fitting tee shirts that revealed his physique. Many girls his age found the tall muscular boy with dark pensive eyes and black wavy hair physically attractive and exciting, but once they learned his true nature the attraction faded. Some, however, enjoyed the pursuit, the attention, and the "bad boy" persona. Many of those fulfilled their own fantasies when they yielded to his physical ultimatums, but once his desires had been satisfied he tossed them aside and moved on to new conquests. A bunch of disillusioned and heartsick females lay in his wake.

The sheriff learned that as Herron got older his appetites developed more perversion and he became more adamant with his degenerate demands. Those revelations worried the sheriff, since the scoundrel apparently had an obsession for Linda Elliott, as evidenced by pictures kept tucked away inside pornographic magazines. What happened to Marcia Leggett when she rebuffed Herron's advances remained paramount in Gil's mind.

* * *

"His own father introduced the kid to porno magazines and films? Sounds like both father and son were real hardcore perverts," Randy asserted.

"You can bet they were," Gil replied. "I wasn't an angel growin' up myself, but some of the stuff we found in his trailer made me blush. Stuff like I ain't never seen before."

"Like what?"

"Oh, you know, hardcore porno magazines, really explicit movies, and weird 'toys'. The thing that bothered me the most was a bunch of pictures of a lot of different girls, but mostly of Marcia and Linda. We found pictures he took from a distance, at different places around town and some . . . well, we don't need to go into that."

"Some what?" Randy insisted.

"Let's just say that he snuck up and peeked through their bedroom windows and snapped pictures at inopportune times. The majority were of Marcia and Linda, but there were a whole bunch like that of other Leadville girls. That's enough said about that. I wouldn't want it to get out that he had naked pictures of so many of the town's young female population. Think just how embarrassin' that would be," Gil responded.

"Yeah, okay. I get the picture. The man was a real creep."

"I kinda thought and hoped that he had left the area, but deep down I had no doubt in my mind but that he would sneak back into town and pursue Linda. I figured he wouldn't quit until he fulfilled his fantasies with her and then he'd move on to one of the other girls."

"Sounds a hair bit risky on his part," Randy asserted. "You'd think he'd be afraid of getting caught especially with the likes of you after 'im."

"The guy was totally nuts," Gil replied. "No logical thought ever entered his perverted mind. The only things he ever thought about was females, what he would do to them, what they could do for him, especially Linda Elliott."

* * *

Herron took on the look of a crazed wild man from way back in the sticks. His dark greasy hair grew down passed his shoulders and a thick black beard covered his face, the result of eight months without a shave or a haircut. The fugitive washed himself as best he could while in exile through the winter, but the lack of water for a real bath left him nasty. His dirty clothes clung to him and a foul stench engulfed his body.

The unrecognizable vagrant walked boldly into the Crews-Beggs Dry Goods store that occupied space on the street level of the Delaware Hotel where the sheriff lived. The horrified store clerk insisted that the vagrant leave, but when the bum flashed money in the man's face the worker became compliant and helped the filthy customer with his purchases. The nasty, smelly man purchased a new pair of Wranglers, a shirt, socks, jockey shorts, and a pair of scissors. He had spent little over the past eight months and he still had most of the pay he had drawn at the Climax Mine.

Gotta get myself cleaned up. Can't go after that Linda gal looking and smelling like I do. She probably wouldn't give me a second glance the way I am, he thought as he brazenly walked north on Harrison

Avenue in broad daylight. *They got pay showers at the washateria up on the north end of town. Gonna trim my hair and beard some, just enough to make 'em neater, but I'm gonna leave it about down to my shoulders and keep my beard. That way, don't think nobody'll know me.*

Back in the day I would have run that guy in for vagrancy, Gil thought as he spotted the long-haired, filthy, bearded stranger who walked along Harrison Avenue in front of the old Tabor Opera House. *But, these days, I can't haul him in for just looking suspicious, much as I'd like to. Don't look like nobody I ever saw around here before.* The sheriff had no idea that the thin-framed unfamiliar person was his suspect, since the heavier built Herron had worn his hair short and had never sported a beard. Once more the fugitive had narrowly escaped capture.

The lack of high caloric foods caused a significant loss of weight while Herron hid out in the mountains through the winter, but the high protein diet from wild game he killed and cooked helped build muscles. The recluse had fanatically exercised each day while in exile under the delusion that Linda had an attraction for him. He did hundreds of push-ups, sit-ups, and used different items as weights that kept his upper body muscled up. The delusional man's appearance had changed drastically, and he fantasized that the girl appreciated a masculine physique, which she did, just not his.

A layer of smelly nasty brownish gunk swirled down the drain in the bottom of the shower as soap and hot water washed away eight months of grime, filth, and stink from Herron's foul form. Clean underwear, socks, breeches, and shirt felt refreshing against the renewed cleanliness of his body. The "new" man retrieved other articles of his clothing from dryers in the laundromat and stuffed them into his backpack. The eight-month accumulation of filth and grunge had disappeared from his body and attire. Pursuit of his conquest lay ahead.

The delusional man imagined that Linda Elliott had no resistance to what he considered his charms, good looks, and physically fit body. *I'll catch her out away from home and we'll go off someplace real private and have us a real good time. Maybe I'll take her up to my favorite spot on Turquoise Lake. Nobody hardly ever goes up there, so we won't be bothered by nobody.*

For several weeks after Herron raped and killed her best friend, Linda Elliott lived in fear that the rapist had designs on her. She appreciated the extra patrols near her home initiated by Sheriff Gentry and she felt comfortable under the constant protection of her father. As weeks passed it seemed to the girl that the danger had subsided, since no further actions by the rapist had taken place. The horror of that infamous night had faded somewhat from her mind and the minds of folks in Lake County. Never permitted any alone time away from home, Linda felt smothered and imprisoned by the relentless surveillance by her relatives and friends. Her family welcomed her female buddies into their home for overnight visits, but they did not allow excursions down Harrison Avenue, the typical activity for teenagers in Leadville.

Linda and her friend, Shannon, completed their homework, giggled as they chatted about different boys they knew, and talked about other girly things while they sat on the porch of the Elliott home. They gazed at the surrounding mountains and the evening sun created a breathtaking horizon as it slowly sank behind Mt. Elbert, a peak that lay to the west of Leadville and towered to over fourteen-thousand feet. With the warm weather, the allure of the setting sun, the call of the mountains, and the desire of association with their friends at the courthouse parking lot the two girls formulated a devious plan.

"After supper and when everybody's gone to sleep, we'll sneak out and go to town," Linda declared. "We'll climb out through my bedroom window and head out."

"Won't your folks hear when you start the truck?" Shannon questioned.

"I got that figured out."

A full moon that glowed brightly in the night sky provided a light that guided Linda across her bedroom to a window that she quietly opened and then removed the screen. The heavenly light created a silhouette of the two friends against a mountain backdrop as they slipped through the opening and headed across the yard to Linda's truck. Linda placed the gear shift in neutral before she and Shannon pushed the vehicle down the inclined driveway to the road. Once out of hearing range they climbed in, started the engine, and drove off toward town. They had escaped.

When Linda drove north on Harrison Avenue she sensed a freedom that she had not experienced for eight months and it felt good. Life had returned to normal for the teenager, or so she thought. Many cars and pickups crowded the courthouse parking lot as the escaped teenaged girls pulled into a space. They observed many of their friends who milled around, gathered in small groups, and talked about school, girlfriends, boyfriends, and other teenaged activities. Some of the "wilder" kids took swigs of whiskey from bottles concealed in brown paper bags, others took hits off marijuana joints, and a few brazenly indulged in activities normally done in private. When the bright sun disappeared behind the massive peaks, the moon appeared in the heavens, and bathed the high mountain town in a soothing light. Everything appeared serene in Lake County, but reprehensible events shattered the illusion.

"Who is that wooly booger with all the girls around him?" Shannon asked as she spotted the group near the courthouse steps. A tall, slim, muscular stranger with shoulder-length black hair and a full beard dominated the attention of the girls that gathered around him.

"I've got no idea," Linda answered. "Don't think I've ever seen him around here before."

"Me either. I think he's kinda creepy looking."

"Oh, come on, Shannon. I think he's kinda cute," Linda asserted. "And look how those muscles ripple. Woo-ee, can't you just imagine those arms holding you tight against his rock-hard abs?"

"Good grief, Linda. I can't believe you'd even think such a thing. Nobody around here wears their hair that long except some of those old hippies out of Denver. Looks like some kinda creep to me. Looks like trouble."

"Well, he ain't no old hippie. I think that beard is kinda sexy and that slim, muscled-up body stuffed into those tight jeans and tee is a real turn-on."

"You would. You think anything wearing pants is sexy," Shannon replied with a smirk.

"Let's go find out who he is."

As the curious girls approached the group, Linda sensed that she knew the long-haired, bearded, muscular young man, but in the excitement of the moment she pushed those feelings to the back of her mind. The predator's excitement accelerated as Linda and Shannon came closer. He carefully concealed his identity and spoke with an accent he had practiced all winter for just such an occasion that now presented itself. His unsuspecting prey had no idea that she now stood in the presence of, and carried on a conversation with the murdering rapist who had raped, tortured, and killed her best friend, Marcia.

* * *

"I cannot believe that Linda didn't recognize Herron," Randy asserted. "I mean, she knew him, she had been to his trailer, and sorta had a confrontation with him the night he raped and killed Marcia."

"She told us that he looked completely different," Gil responded. "She said he had slimmed down and muscled up, and looked real sexy—her words, not mine! He had been clean shaven with short hair, but now sported a beard and long hair."

"What finally clued her in?" Randy asked.

"The fake accent. She told us it didn't sound real," Gil answered. "Nobody around here talked like he did."

* * *

"Howdy, y'all, bless your hearts, y'all look so sweet," Herron greeted when Linda and Shannon joined the group.

"You sure talk funny," Linda noted.

"Bless your pea-pickin' heart, gal, it's 'cause I hail from Texas," he responded, but Linda had met many tourists who had come to Colorado from all parts of the Lone Star State and she had never heard a Texan that sounded like he did. She figured the stranger just adopted a strange persona and thought it made an impression on the girls. Many in the group fell for the masquerade.

Although Linda had an attraction for the weird stranger, her cautious side kicked in. "Come on, Shannon. I think we'd better go back home."

"Oh, come on, Linda. We just got here. You're no fun."

"Something just doesn't feel right about that weird guy who claims to be from Texas. You stay here if you want to, but I'm going home."

"Just a little while ago you thought he was cute and sexy," Shannon reminded.

"That was before I got a close up look at 'im and heard that fake accent. Something is wrong here. I'm going home."

Go ahead, party pooper," Shannon responded. "I'll get somebody to bring me back out to your place later."

Engrossed in normal teenaged chit-chat and mellowed out from the joint they passed around, no one noticed when Herron left the group and followed the object of his obsession as she headed to her pickup. *Bam!* He slammed her truck door shut, and Linda dropped her keys when she felt an arm that grabbed her about the waist, whirled her around, and shoved her up hard against the vehicle. The assailant pressed his body against hers. The unexpected action caused a surge of exhilaration that coursed through her body, but the fright that also entered her mind overruled her excitement.

"What are you doing?" she asked as she stiffened up and pushed him away. "Who are you anyway?"

"Lighten up, Linda. You know what I want, and I know you want it too," he exclaimed without the fake accent.

"What are you talking about?" the teenager asked with an air of naivete as she thought, *I know that voice from somewhere.*

"You know what I'm talking about. I know an isolated spot up close to Turquoise Lake. We can go up there where it's real private, or we can go on to Emerald Lake. It's real secluded. Only people ever go there is fishermen and there won't be none this time of night, so nobody'd bother us. I got a bottle of Jack, we can have a shot, smoke a little dope, get real loose, have ourselves a real good time, and do some 'fishing' of our own. Know what I mean?" the scoundrel suggested as he pulled Linda close and boldly kissed her.

"HELP! HELP! HELP ME!" She screamed. The frightened girl realized the true identity of the stranger, shoved him away with all her strength, and ran toward her friends.

The group heard her frantic plea and rushed in her direction. *Swoosh!* Linda's pickup almost hit the teenagers as Herron who had retrieved Linda's keys that she dropped, drove it past them and headed out on Harrison Avenue.

"What's happening," Shannon asked. "Who was that?"

"Oh my God. It's . . . it's Richard Herron, the one that murdered

Marcia. Somebody call the sheriff," Linda instructed as she slumped to the ground in an emotional collapse. "Oh, God! He came back for me. Wanted me to go with him. He was gonna rape me too, and probably woulda killed me."

* * *

"Boy, she was one lucky girl," Randy declared. "She could have been killed."

"She was that," Katy injected.

"For sure," Gil responded. "The excitement of the new stranger in town and of the unknown almost lured her into a life-threatening situation."

"I can't believe the idiot came back to Leadville and tried it again," Randy exclaimed. "You woulda thought he'd 'a known that somebody would figure out who he was."

"I told you, he was a complete nutcase. He thought no one would recognize him with long hair and a beard."

"Good thing she figured out who he was before she got in the pickup with him."

* * *

Gil arrived on the scene a few minutes later, dispersed the teenaged crowd, and drove Linda and Shannon back to the Elliott home. The murdering rapist had brazenly returned to Leadville and had almost repeated the horrific crime. Winter had passed, snow had melted, and summer loomed near. The chase resumed.

CHAPTER 10

THE RENEWED CHASE

As the renewal of spring bathed Lake County in warm sunshine and as summer drew near, Gil Gentry also experienced a renewed vigor in his pursuit of the murdering rapist, Richard Herron. Although the sheriff had pursued numerous leads on horseback during the winter, the ice, deep snow, and impassable roads made the search for the fugitive nearly impossible. A brutally cold season had been the predator's friend, but not so spring and summer. The unrelenting lawman vowed capture and incarceration of the killer before the cold icy precipitation engulfed the area once again.

He realized that the fugitive's mode of operation had probably changed with the season. Gil assumed that Herron had holed up in one place over the winter, but figured he most likely had moved on from where ever that hideout may have been. He assumed that, in all probability, the elusive lunatic relocated from place to place as a defense against capture.

The sheriff had stationed deputies at the Elliott home around the clock since he realized the obsession held by Herron clouded what little sense of right or wrong he may have had. Gil figured that the isolation of winter had intensified the scoundrel's unholy desires that involved Linda. Even at the risk of capture he expected the return of the predator and a rekindled effort for fulfillment of his atrocious fantasies. The horrific events of the previous year played like a bad movie in the lawman's mind as he drove south on Harrison Avenue toward the home of Herron's next intended victim. Visions of Marcia's burned and mutilated body tortured Gil's soul, and a picture of the glove of skin swirled about in his thoughts.

It happened once, but I will not let that happen to Linda or any other girl in my county, Gil thought as he pulled in the driveway of the Elliott home. When he arrived, Gil relieved the officer on duty and asked Linda's father's permission for an interview with the girl.

"Don't want to alarm you, but with all the snow gone and warm weather comin', I'm afraid Herron might come back again," Gil declared.

"You think so? You don't think he'd be afraid of gettin' caught?"

"The guy is nuts, just plain crazy, and I think he'd do anything to get what he wants," the sheriff answered. "I believe what he wants is Linda."

"He shows up around here, I'll blow 'im to kingdom come," the father informed as he stroked a 12-gauge shotgun that stood near the door.

"And I wouldn't blame you and that's exactly what you should do if he shows up and tries anything with Linda. That would save a lot time and trouble, but hopefully we'll catch the sorry devil and let the system handle it. I need to talk to Linda if it's okay with you, Mr. Elliott."

"Sure, Sheriff," the father answered. "Whatever we can do to help catch the S.O.B. Come on in the kitchen, got a pot of coffee on the stove. Ask Linda whatever you need to."

"Thanks," the sheriff replied as he sat at the kitchen table and took a swig of the strong black coffee.

"Tell me everything that happened last night," Gil instructed as Linda entered the room and sat at the table across from him. "Don't leave anything out. The smallest little detail might just be the clue we need to find 'im."

"I'm sorry, Sheriff," Linda responded as tears streamed down her cheeks. "I just can't talk about it. I just can't. When I realized who he was and what he probably had in mind for me I was so scared. It's just too upsetting."

"I know it's hard," Gil assured with the warmth of understanding.

"Linda, you've got to tell Sheriff Gentry about it," her father insisted. "He's got to catch 'im so he can't come back and hurt you or any other girl."

"Just take your time. Tell me what he looked like. Try to remember everything he said," Gil urged.

"Okay, I'll do my best," Linda conceded.

As the intended victim gave the sheriff a detailed description of the long-haired, bearded Herron, Gil blurted out. "Oh, my God. I saw a guy that matches that description walking up Harrison Avenue yesterday morning. The guy I saw was filthy dirty. Looked like he hadn't had a bath in months and his hair hung way down past his shoulders and looked like you could squeeze grease out of it."

"Probably a different guy. Herron was real clean. Had on clothes that looked brand new," Linda informed. "His hair came down to his shoulders, but not past them and it wasn't greasy at all. Even though it was long, it was neat and clean. I really thought he was kinda cute and sexy until I figured out who he was."

Linda's father shot her a disapproving stare. "Linda! Sheriff Gentry don't want to hear talk like that."

"I'm sorry, Daddy, but he did look kinda cute, and whether you like it or not, girls do think about boys as more than brothers."

"Don't want to hear such talk," the father responded. "Sorry, Sheriff."

"It's okay, Mr. Elliott. Linda needs to tell me everything."

"Even though I was kinda attracted to him, things just didn't feel right."

"I'd bet the guy I saw was Herron," Gil asserted. "Lot of campers and other folks go to the washateria up at the north end of town to take a shower. That's the only place around here where they have pay showers except up at Honey Loaf."

"All I know is he was clean and was wearing new clothes," Linda replied.

"Did he say anything, anything at all that might give me a clue where he might be headed?"

"He wanted to take me up to . . . Turq . . . Turquoise Lake," she sobbed as thoughts of her raped and murdered friend engulfed her mind.

"Good grief! He was gonna take you where he . . ." Gil stopped, and did not finish the statement.

"That's right. He was gonna take me to the same place where he raped and murdered Marcia. Probably woulda done the same to me. Scares the crap out of me when I think about what he had in mind," Linda sobbed as she wiped tears from her eyes. "What if he comes back for me?"

"We're gonna keep a deputy on guard here until we catch 'im. In the meantime, do not go anywhere by yourself," Gil instructed.

"Thank you, Sheriff," the father responded. "Makes me feel a lot better with one of your guys around."

"Anything else you can think of, Linda?"

"He mentioned taking me someplace else further up in the mountains. Can't remember what he called it, but he talked about some little lake and he mentioned fishing."

"Emerald Lake?" Gil questioned.

"Yes, that's it. He said nobody goes up there except fishermen and he said if one of them got in the way he'd take care of 'em."

"Sounds like he woulda . . ." Gil stopped. He did not want to upset Linda further.

* * *

"I coulda kicked myself all over Lake County," Gil declared regretfully. "Twice, not once, but twice I'd had a chance to get my hands on Herron, and I just let 'im go about his business."

"You had no way of knowing," Randy assured.

"Yeah, but I shoulda followed my gut instincts like I usually do. Damn it! I just let the bastard slip through my fingers."

"There you go with the language again," Katy scolded.

"I'm sorry, darlin', but it just makes me so mad. I wanted to help kids. That's one reason I became a lawman, but I failed the kids of Lake County, especially Marcia, and I damn near failed Linda too."

"You did not." Katy affirmed.

"Yeah, Gil. Quit beating yourself up. How could you have known what he was gonna do?" Randy questioned.

"Shoulda had a better handle on what was going on in my county."

"Cut it out. There was no way you coulda known," Katy asserted.

* * *

"I reckon I'll take a ride up to that spot at Turquoise Lake, look around, and see if there are any signs of him up there."

"You be careful, Sheriff. Like you said, he is nuts. He's just crazy enough, he might shoot you. He hasn't got anything to lose," Elliott asserted.

"Oh, you can bet I'll be on my toes. If I don't find him at Turquoise, then I'll run on up to Emerald Lake see what I can find. Linda, if you think of anything else, call the office and they'll get ahold of me."

As soon as another deputy arrived at the Elliott home, Gil headed toward Turquoise Lake, the scene of the original crime, and apparently one of the intended spots for a second offense.

Majestic pine and towering aspen blocked most of the sun's rays and cast shadows that created an eerie picture of the area where the sheriff had visited several times since that fateful night. In search of what, he did not know. He knew the identity of the perpetrator and nothing at the scene ever furnished any clue as to his whereabouts. Some force continually called the sheriff back to the place, and the lawman feared he had missed some clue. The spot became known as the most gruesome site in Lake County, and many folks thought Marcia's spirit remained there. Gil put no credence in such speculation and the logical man sloughed off his own feelings when he felt her surreal presence all around him at the location.

The lawman kept his eyes peeled as he walked down the hill into the ravine where he found Marcia's tan breeches and white tennis shoes. He climbed up to the top of the rise on the other side where Herron's white briefs had been located, in search of anything that pertained to the murdering rapist. The sheriff found no evidence that the fugitive had been there in recent days, so he abandoned the search.

He returned to his squad car, and headed up the mountain toward Emerald Lake. More suited for a four-wheel drive vehicle, the road to the small body of water narrowed and became almost impassable for the squad car. Low-lying tree branches screeched as they scraped the side of the Ford Crown Victoria, and dust from the dirt road infiltrated the cabin of the automobile. *Shoulda come in the Land Cruiser,* Gil thought as he wondered why anybody braved those conditions, when he recollected the many fishermen who frequented the place. He did remember, however, the plentiful trout in the azure waters of the lake. The sheriff recalled the few times he had fished there, each time he threw a line in the crystal-clear, cold water, one of the fish struck the bait, and he had a catch. Most anglers caught their limit of the appropriate size in a period of no more than two hours. Gil knew Herron's background as an avid outdoorsman and he figured Emerald Lake furnished the fugitive with sustenance.

When Gil reached the little-used camping area about one-half mile from the water, he discovered that the heavy snows and ice of the previous season had completely blocked the road. Trees that had come crashing down from the weight of the accumulation barricaded the lane. He parked the squad car at one of the campsites and the ever-vigilant lawman kept a watchful eye out for any sign of Herron as he walked the rugged trail toward the lake. He recalled that Linda told him that Herron wore work boots and fresh tracks in the occasional patches of soft dirt told him that someone with similar footwear had walked the path in the last twenty-four hours. Gil noted that the imprints only headed in the direction of the lake and he spotted none going the opposite way. If the tracks belonged to Herron, he most likely remained somewhere in the vicinity.

Smoke hung low in the heavily wooded area near the lake and Gil caught a whiff of burning wood as he trudged along the path to the water's edge. *Maybe I'm gonna get lucky today and catch 'im,* the sheriff thought as he pulled his gun from its holster and proceeded quietly across the rough terrain through a thick layer of pine needles toward the campfire.

"Sorry, guys," the anxious lawman apologized as he quickly returned the pistol to the holster when he spotted a group of fishermen who sat around the fire.

"Hell, Gil. We thought you was gonna shoot us," one man who knew the sheriff declared.

"How's the fishin'?" Gil questioned.

"You gonna shoot the fish with that gun?" another man asked with a chuckle. "Done limited out. Thought we'd cook up a few for lunch before we head out."

"Yeah, right. I know you guys. Thought you'd eat up the

116

evidence and then fish some more. Pretty sneaky," the sheriff accused jokingly.

"What are you doing up this way, Sheriff?"

"Looking for the fugitive, Richard Herron," Gil answered. "You know, the one that raped and murdered the Leggett girl last year."

"Good grief. You think he might be up this way somewhere?"

"He mentioned Emerald Lake to another intended victim just last night. Y'all seen anybody round these parts?" The sheriff asked as he related a description of Herron to the fishermen.

"Oh, my God, Sheriff. He was right here. You missed 'im by about four hours."

"What do you mean?" Gill asked.

"He was right here at this very spot when we got here," another fisherman informed. "Acted kinda skittish when he saw us. Never said a word. Just got up and took off through the woods."

"Y'all are real lucky. This guy is armed and desperate. I think he would kill anybody he thought might be a threat."

"Damn it, Gil. You're scaring the hell out of me."

"Since y'all have already limited out, I think I'd get on out of here. Which way was he headed?" the sheriff inquired.

"Back toward the road, but he went up through the trees and stayed off the trail."

Gil headed out through the forest in the direction indicated by the fishermen, he noted disturbances in the pine needles, and he spotted boot prints in the soft dirt where no debris covered the ground. The tracker followed the trail and it led back to near where he had parked the squad car. The sharp-eyed sheriff followed the boot prints to a campsite not far from his car and there he observed tire tracks. Herron had either hitched a ride with an unsuspecting motorist or he had stolen himself a set of wheels. The lawman feared that some clueless good Samaritan may have been harmed or even killed by the fugitive. He knew the desperate Herron had no hesitation about hurting anything or anybody who stood in his way.

Upon Gil's return arrival at his office he observed a highly-agitated man with a bloody face who stood on the steps of the courthouse. The injured citizen related a story of a carjacking and assault as he mopped blood from his face with a handkerchief. "I'd just parked my truck up close to Emerald Lake. Was getting my fishing gear out of the back when this long-haired guy came out of the woods and pointed a gun at me. Scared the crap out of me. He made me get in the driver's seat and drive him to town. Said if I didn't do what he told me he'd shoot me."

"Yeah, and he would have, too," Gil asserted. "You're one lucky dude."

"He had me drive him to the north edge of town and then he hit me up the side of my head with the barrel of his gun and shoved me out of the truck and took off."

"Headed north?" Gil asked.

"Yeah, said something about some place near Red Cliff. The maniac mumbled something about hell, or hail, or maybe Hale. He was plumb wired, kinda crazy like. Babbled on and on about some girl named Linda. Swore she'd give 'im what he wanted, or she'd regret it. He was a lunatic, higher 'n a kite."

"Sounds like more than a marijuana high to me," Gil asserted. "More like he was high on meth or cocaine instead of bein' stoned on weed."

"Probably. His eyes weren't droopy or sleepy-looking like I've heard that marijuana does. They were wild and crazed."

"Most likely he was high on meth. The drugs kinda betrayed 'im, loosened up his tongue. He was probably talking about Camp Hale, that abandoned army training camp 'bout halfway between here and Vail close to Red Cliff in Eagle County. He may be planning on holdin' up in the ruins of some of the old buildin's. I'll get one of my deputies to take you to the hospital and get that gash on your head taken care of. I'm headin' up toward Vail. See if I can catch up to 'im."

* * *

"For the third time—the third time—I had come real close," Gil lamented. "It was like some evil force was keepin' him one step ahead of me."

"Yeah, but I know how dogged stubborn you are, Uncle Gil. You weren't about to give up the chase."

"Hell, no, I wasn't. I was gonna catch that murderin' rapist pervert if it took me the rest of my life."

"That sounds like the Gil Gentry I know," Randy asserted.

"I wasn't gonna rest 'til I shot him dead myself or I saw 'em stick the needle to 'im."

"And that finally happened," Katy injected.

"Yeah, I'm glad I lived to see it, but it didn't bring Marcia back. She's still out there in the cemetery."

CHAPTER 11

THE CONTINUED CHASE

As Gil drove north on Highway 24 he lamented that the murdering rapist had placed a blemish on the reputation of Leadville and the picturesque scenery around the town. Prior to the horrific crime, Leadville had been a mecca for tourists, campers, and fishermen. Families had flocked to the area to enjoy the beauty nature had bestowed on the landscape. The crystal-clear azure waters of the numerous trout-filled lakes and nightly melodramas performed at the historic Tabor Opera House lured many visitors to the area. Fear of the evil that lurked somewhere in the mountains diminished the normal flow of people to the town and surrounding countryside full of history.

Several diehard anglers fished along the banks of a small lake on the north side of the highway. A locomotive slowed down as it rounded a curve and chugged by on rails that ran along the mountainside on the south. Smoke from the engine that swirled around in the clean mountain air and hung low over the body of water in the high valley created a peaceful scenic atmosphere.

The offensive smell of diesel-fuel better represented the emotional upheaval experienced by folks in the area. No amount of tranquility prevailed so long as Herron remained on the loose. Residents locked doors that had normally remained unlocked and windows that had usually allowed nature's air conditioning into homes remained shut and secured. Most inhabitants slept with loaded guns close at hand.

Located in rugged mountainous country north of Leadville near Red Cliff, at 9200 feet above sea level in the Eagle River Valley, Camp Hale had served as a training base for the U.S. Army 10th Mountain Division. As hostilities increased and World War II escalated, instructors trained men in Alpine skiing, mountain climbing, and winter survival as preparation for deployment to similar terrain overseas. The camp later served as a prisoner of war detention center and housed around four hundred German captives. Ruins of the old field house buildings on the grounds may have supplied shelter for the fugitive. Reports of unexploded ordnance that dated back to the war gave the area a reputation of extreme danger. Gil approached the site with intense caution.

I've got 'im now, Gil thought as he parked the squad car next to a pickup truck that met the description given by Herron's carjack victim. The driver's side door remained ajar and as the sheriff investigated he found items that apparently belonged to the fugitive. A pornographic magazine lay on the seat opened to a disgustingly explicit picture and the smell of marijuana that permeated the air irritated the sheriff's senses. Gil figured capture of the scoundrel loomed near as he realized the man's fear of apprehension must have diminished somewhat when he took time for a hit off a joint, a gaze at his favorite "reading" material, and the activity that accompanied it.

In recent years, Camp Hale had become a developmental training center where disadvantaged youth had exposure to some of the same challenges as the army trainees. The instructors of the group knew which spots had been cleared of ordnance and only used those areas for their routine with the kids. Gil feared that if the fugitive came into contact with the youngsters, and in his desperate state of mind, considered them a threat, he might harm them. The sheriff worried about the safety of young innocent bystanders if Herron initiated a fire fight. To his great relief, upon inquiry at the center's headquarters Gil learned from the leader of the program that no sessions had been scheduled for that day.

"If he's up to it, have a deputy bring the carjack victim out here to Camp Hale," Gil instructed the dispatcher. "Tell 'um to fingerprint the truck, bag anything that probably belongs to Herron, and then release the vehicle to the owner. I know he needs his wheels and there isn't any reason to impound it."

"Will do, Boss," the dispatcher responded. "You be careful up there. Herron'd just as soon shoot you as not and watch out for those live ordnances. There's a lot of them still up there. You know we've had numerous accidents up there from the live ammo."

"Wouldn't it be just too damn bad if one of those old munitions blew Herron to kingdom come? Gil suggested. "You know me. Mr. cautious.".

"Yeah, right. I can see it now, you just charging in with guns a-blazing. You be careful."

"I think I'm close to gettin' him. He's probably hold up in some of the ruins."

"I hope so. Everybody hereabouts will breathe easier when he's behind bars."

"Yeah, or pushin' up daisies," Gil replied.

That damn sheriff just won't give it up, Herron thought as he spotted Gil when the sheriff parked next the stolen pickup. The fugitive hid behind a huge bolder close to the parking area and there he remained, still, and quiet. *It appears that he's headed to the old ruins to look for me. That'll take a while so as soon as he's out of sight I'll jump in the pickup and get the hell out of here.*

When Gil disappeared into the woods, Herron approached the stolen vehicle, but to his chagrin he discovered that the sheriff had removed the keys. *Woo, woo,* he heard the locomotive whistle and smelled the smoke from the diesel engine as it rounded the sharp curve. The fugitive grabbed his backpack, and headed across the highway toward the tracks. The train reduced speed as it chugged around the bend and the fugitive reached up and grabbed the edge of the opening in an empty boxcar. In the struggle as he pulled himself onto the conveyance, the backpack that contained his clothing, dope, and "reading" material slipped from his back and fell to the ground.

Ah, hell, Herron thought as he lifted himself into the boxcar. *There goes my clean drawers, my weed, and worst of all my magazines. I can do without my drawers—who needs 'em anyhow—and I can rip off more reads in town, but I got no way to get more dope.*

With his gun at the ready, Gil moved silently through the pine and aspen as he approached the remains of the old field house. The lawman hid behind the large trees and surveyed the area through binoculars. When he detected no movement in the ruins he camouflaged himself behind the timber, ran in a crouched position from one large tree or boulder to another. After he repeated the process several times, the sheriff stood behind the first wall of the old building. Gil thought of the many men who had trained at the facility. Brave men who had fought in foreign lands for preservation of freedom. He recalled them with appreciation as he observed the structure that stood at the base of a mountain summit and stretched out approximately one hundred feet. Eight walls of concrete stood about fifteen or sixteen feet apart and created seven separate spaces tied together with large concrete beams at the peak.

The stealthy enforcer of the law pointed his Smith and Wesson .44 Magnum forward as he moved from one section of the old ruins to another until he had cleared each space. If the fugitive had holed up there, he had now vacated the area and moved on. Gil kept his eyes peeled for unexploded munitions as he searched wooded areas and clearings over the next couple of hours. He found no evidence of Herron's presence, no boot prints in patches of soft dirt, no disturbances of pine needles, and no broken or mashed down weeds or greasewood. Apparently, the rat had escaped capture one more time.

When Gil abandoned the search of the Camp Hale property and returned to his squad car, he glanced across the road and observed something that seemed totally out of place along the railroad track. Upon closer investigation, he realized that a backpack lay beside the rails. Inside the bag, he found numerous pornographic publications, some with pictures of Linda Elliott tucked inside, and a fair quantity of marijuana. Once again, the fugitive had remained one step ahead of the lawman. Gil assumed that the scoundrel had hopped aboard a freight train when it slowed down at the sharp curve in the line.

Might as well head back to town, Gil thought as he collected the backpack and returned to his car. *He's got several hours head start and that train slows down at every curve so he could'a jumped off anywhere along the route. I'll keep my eyes open, but he could be anywhere.*

"You guys seen anybody like that?" Gil asked as he described Herron to the fishermen at the small lake.

"Yep," one of the anglers replied. "A man that looked just like you described stood in plain sight in one of the empty boxcars when the train passed by several hours back."

* * *

"Just seemed like the devil himself was protectin' Herron," Gil asserted. "I kept gettin' real close, but he out foxed me ever time. What the hell kind of lawman was I anyhow?"

"A good one," Katy responded. "You never gave up until you caught him."

"Yeah, and that's what counts," Randy added.

"But, still. It took too damn long. Time and again I let him slip through my fingers and people were gettin' hurt. It was like Herron was thumbin' his nose at me. Kinda symbolically giving me the finger."

"I see what you mean," Randy responded. "Think I woulda felt the same, but you did apprehend him in the end."

"You ain't heard nothin' yet," Gil assured. "That very night he was real close and one more time I screwed up. Let him get away without a chase."

"What are you talking about?" Randy asked.

* * *

The distraught lawman tossed and turned throughout the night as he sought sleep and respite from the day's events. Again, visions of Marcia's raped, mutilated, and burned body filled his thoughts and fears of attacks on more girls haunted him. His mind conjured up pictures of a bullet fired from his own gun that flew through the air in slow motion before it hit the rapist right between the eyes, splattering blood and brains all around. He also envisioned the needle administered by the executioner that ended the murderer's life. Just as the restless soul almost fell asleep, an unidentifiable sound echoed from the first floor of the old Delaware Hotel where Gil rented a room. The noise sounded like the crash of breaking glass, but it did not reverberate loudly, and in his groggy state Gil brushed it off, rolled over, and continued his quest for rest.

Bam! Bam! Bam! Gil sat up on the side of the bed as he heard the noise when someone banged at his door. A quick glance at the alarm clock that sat on the nightstand next to his bed told him that he had slept much later than usual. "Who is it?" he shouted as he headed across the room to the door.

125

"It's Crystal from the Mine Shaft Bookstore." A unique bookstore occupied a small space next to the dry goods store on the first floor of the Delaware.

"Hang on, I'll be right there," Gil instructed as he grabbed his pants from the chair where they lay, pulled them on, and opened the door.

"I saw your car in your parking place and figured you were still here, so I came straight to you instead of calling in," Crystal informed.

"Callin' in about what?"

"Somebody broke the glass out of the front door of the store sometime in the night," she reported.

"Oh, damn. That's what I heard just about the time I almost fell asleep," the sheriff responded. "Did they steal anything?"

"That's what's real odd. They didn't bother anything except the adult magazine section. Took every one of 'em. Didn't take the money from the register or anything else. Just the magazines."

"Did you touch or move anything?" Gil asked.

"No, just as soon as I realized I'd been robbed I came straight to you."

"Good. Don't touch nothin'. I'll be down there just as soon as I finish gettin' dressed."

The sheriff called his office and requested a deputy with fingerprinting equipment be sent to the book store. Just as Crystal had described, glass shards littered the sidewalk and the floor inside the busted door and the missing publications appeared as the only items disturbed.

It seemed to Gil that it took forever, but just as he suspected, when the fingerprint report came back from Denver several days later it identified Richard Herron as the perpetrator who smashed the front door of the Mine Shaft Bookstore and lifted all the risqué reading material.

That weirdo just couldn't do without his readin' material, *but I know Crystal doesn't stock any of the hardcore stuff.* Playboy *isn't explicit enough to satisfy the pervert and will only agitate him,* Gil thought. *He could be long gone, or he could still be right here someplace. Who knows, but I'd bet he's still close by, just waitin' for a chance to abduct Linda. That ain't gonna happen.*

Every available deputy and city police officers patrolled the streets of Leadville, the highways, and the backroads of Lake County. They kept the Elliott home under constant surveillance for fear the obsessed rapist planned implementation of his plot against Linda. Weeks passed with no sign of the wanted murderer and law enforcement eventually assumed he had cleared out of the area.

Sheriff Gentry sat at his desk in deep concentration and contemplated his next move in the search for Richard Herron. The loud irritating ring of the phone interrupted his thought processes. "Sheriff, this is Ray at the Healy House. We've had a break-in."

An elegant three-story Victorian home built by August Meyer in 1878, the Healy House remained in near pristine condition as a museum with many artifacts original to the house or from the same era. A Sears and Roebuck catalogue lay opened on the kitchen table and reflected what seemed as ridiculously low prices for products of the day. Re-enactors who dressed in period clothing and spoke in the vernacular of the times acted as guides for tourists when they visited. The residence operated for some time as a boarding house and it is assumed that it got its name from Dan Healy and his cousin Nellie, boarders who resided at the establishment.

"Anything missin'?" Gil questioned.

"Not that I can determine," Ray answered. "Just a broken window in one of the doors and a Murphy bed in one of the bedrooms was opened up and apparently, someone slept there."

"Anything else?"

"Odd, but there was a copy of *Playboy* magazine left on the bed with the name *Linda* scrawled out across the young woman pictured in the centerfold. Maybe my imagination but she looks a lot like Linda Elliott and it's covered in some kind'a gooey sticky stuff."

"Don't touch anything," the sheriff instructed as he realized that the break-in had been perpetrated by Richard Herron. He figured the residue was the same as what they found on the aspen leaves at the cemetery. "We'll be right over."

Time passed slowly for Gil as he waited for several days before he received results from Denver of the finger-printing. The outcomes showed Herron's prints all over the broken door, the Murphy bed, and the *Playboy* magazine.

"Herron is back!" Gil exclaimed.

* * *

"It was like he was darin' me to try and catch 'im," Gil declared. "The name Linda scrawled across the *Playboy* centerfold. DNA testin' was almost nonexistent in 1980, but testin' done on the sticky residue lifted from the *Playboy* and Linda's picture years later showed it came from Herron. The S.O.B. was tauntin' me."

"Yeah, you'd think he would'a hightailed it clean out of the area," Randy responded.

"You would think," Gil added. "But, he just either never left or kept comin' back. I think he had two things in mind: he desperately wanted to have his way with Linda Elliott. Nothin' else would satisfy the pervert and I think he probably got off on the torturin' and killin' as much or more than the sex. Secondly, I think he got some kind'a sadistic pleasure out of tauntin' me."

"He didn't know you like I do or he would'a skedaddled clean out of Colorado," Katy injected.

"Yep, dogged stubborn," Randy added. "You weren't about to

stop until you caught im."

"Or shot 'im dead," Gil suggested. "I know I shouldn't been thinkin' like that, but I just couldn't help myself."

* * *

After the break-in at the Healy House, the Sheriff's Department increased patrols throughout the area and continued its close watch on the Elliott family. Gil knew in his heart and soul that the madman's depraved mind received no satisfaction from anything other than an attack on Linda. The evidence collected at the museum especially the centerfold picture with Linda's name scrawled across it corroborated Gil's analysis of the pervert's motivation.

Apprehension of the murdering rapist consumed Gil Gentry. In pursuit of the felon, the sheriff scoured the city and the countryside by day and considered future options as he lay in bed at night. Images of the horrific crime filled his dreams, his nightmares. Nothing short of capture and execution would bring him peace, or any measure of justice for Marcia Leggett.

CHAPTER 12

THE CAPTURE

Gil searched mountain peaks, valleys, abandoned cabins, and long-ago closed-down mines throughout the summer of 1980 with no success. He followed many tips and leads, but none led him to Herron. The sheriff figured that his pursuit of the fugitive had been temporarily halted when the aspen turned to a golden hue and brisk north winds along with an occasional dusting of snow descended on the area in late September. The smaller than normal flow of tourists had moved on and Leadville had returned to its sleepy little mountain town persona. Winter tourism in Lake County dwindled as most visitors in the snowy months frequented Vail, Breckenridge, or other areas where ski slopes furnished winter activities.

* * *

"Everything was pretty quiet in Leadville," Gil noted. "All the tourists had left, that is all but one real stupid guy and his wife."

"What do you mean, stupid?" Randy questioned.

"The idiot should have cleared out just like all the rest."

"Did that make him 'stupid' just because he didn't leave?"

"Hell, no. There was more that put him in the 'stupid' category," Gil answered. "If they gave an award for 'stupid' he woulda got it."

* * *

130

Typical tourists, Ned, his wife, Lana, and their little dog, Prissy, frequented the Leadville area at least once a year. Although days attained a degree of warmth, the couple enjoyed the cool mountain climate when they visited in the summer months, but in 1980 they came in late September. Ned referred to the state as "Coolarado" since it furnished a respite from the heat of Texas where he and Lana lived. The visitors loved the mountains and many times they explored the back country, traversing the peaks and valleys on roads normally navigated with four-wheel drive vehicles. One isolated spot high up above Tabor's Matchless Mine and the mining district fascinated the couple. A clear cold stream meandered through the high tundra and lush green native grasses grew head high in the area. Vastly different from their everyday lives in the flatlands of Texas, peace and tranquility flowed through their spirits as they sat on the side of the mountain, gazed at the vast picturesque scene, and listened to the soothing ripple of the brook.

The sound of a vehicle interrupted the calming scene as the couple looked at the vastness of the Rocky Mountain range. A late model Chevy pickup roared up the narrow lane and parked near the water not far from the couple's custom van. A man who looked kind of wild-eyed and rather unsavory with shoulder-length hair, a full beard, and dirty clothes emerged from the sparkling clean white truck.

"I think we'd better get the heck out of here," Ned asserted as the unwanted intruder lit a joint of marijuana, pulled a handgun from his waistband, and fired in the air.

"Probably so," Lana responded as the concerned couple moved rapidly toward their vehicle.

"Doesn't seem like he's even aware that we're here."

"Hope it stays like that until we're gone," Lana added in a low voice.

"We've got another carjacking," the sheriff's dispatcher announced over the radio as Gil patrolled the back roads of the county in search of the desperado. "Description fits Herron. Got his self a brand-new show room fresh white Chevy Silverado this time."

"Did he hurt the victim?" Gil asked.

"Thankfully no. Not this time. Oh, and we've got a stranded tourist and his wife up on the road above the mining district. Got two tore-up tires on their custom van."

"What kind of idiot drives a van on that road? It's littered with jagged rocks and boulders the size of a car, barely passable in a four-wheel drive."

Ned and Lana wanted as much distance as possible between them and the grizzly-looking, gun-toting intruder, so they rapidly headed down the rough road toward town. In his haste, the driver hit several sharp rough rocks and ripped two tires into shreds.

"Now what do we do?" Ned questioned. "Only got one spare."

"I suppose we'll have to walk down the mountain into town and get some help," Lana answered.

"But it's a long way to town and it'll be rough hiking, besides I hate to leave the van. That character we saw just might vandalize it looking to steal anything he might could sell for dope money."

"What would you do if he did break into the van with us in it?"

"Got my .22. Reckon I'd have to shoot 'im," Ned asserted boldly.

"You think you could do that?"

"Never had occasion to do so, but if someone threatened you or me, yep, I could do it."

As the couple contemplated their next move the welcoming sound of another vehicle gave them hope of rescue. They also feared it might be another hooligan like the one who smoked dope at the top of the mountain, maybe even his friend. Their fears vanished when a couple that looked compassionate and friendly emerged from a four-wheel drive jeep, a vehicle suited for back roads.

"Looks like you guys have got a real big problem," the young man declared.

"Yep, didn't just tear up one tire, had to tear up two. Only got one spare."

"Y'all hop in the Jeep and we'll take you to town. You can get help there."

"I really don't want to leave the van. There's a real rough-looking character up the road a piece, smoking dope and firing a gun."

"Suit yourself, but if it was me, I want to get the heck out of here, but if you're hell-bent on staying with your van, we'll head back to town and notify the sheriff's office of your predicament. They'll send help."

"Appreciate it," Ned responded. "You guys are life savers."

"Y'all be real careful. I heard there's a murdering rapist hiding out somewhere in these mountains."

As the jeep drove out of sight, Prissy paced back and forth nervously when Ned and Lana got in the van, locked the door, retrieved the gun, and waited for help. Snow flurries descended on the area as the couple shivered from the cold, snuggled together for warmth, and awaited rescue. The husband peered out the side window when he heard a vehicle as it passed by. He observed the same white Chevy truck headed down the mountain in an erratic manner. It repeatedly swerved from one side of the road to the other. The pickup nearly sideswiped the van as though the driver didn't even see it, and almost plummeted off the mountain. After what seemed an eternity, the extremely stressed couple knew assistance had arrived when they spotted a large tow truck as it approached. A Toyota Land Cruiser with Sheriff's Department logo on the door followed behind the wrecker.

"Had a hell of a time getting this big truck up that road. Snow didn't help none either," the tow truck driver declared. "What the hell are y'all doing up here in that van? Anybody with half a brain knows better than to drive a vehicle like that on these roads. Boy, you got less than half a brain?"

"Leave 'em alone," Gil instructed. "They're just a couple of greenhorn tourists."

"Just had to give 'em a little bit of a hard-time. I love folks like them. They're my bread and butter," he declared good-naturedly. "We'll get the van down to the tire shop and they'll get you fixed up."

Ned took no offense at the ribbing since he realized that the man and the sheriff sized them up correctly. Relief at the rescue represented the only emotion in the "greenhorn's" thoughts.

"Understand y'all saw some long-haired dude smoking dope up the road," Gil noted.

"That's right. Looked like weed to me and that sickening bittersweet smell pretty much confirmed it," Ned replied. "He acted plumb crazy, firing a gun in the air, doing other things that Lana did not need to see, and it didn't seem like he even knew we were there."

"Don't want to scare you, but if it's who I think it is you folks are real lucky to still be alive."

"Good God. What do you mean, lucky to be alive?" Ned gasped.

"The guy raped and murdered a teenaged girl from Leadville a year back. Doused her with gas and set her on fire while she was still alive. If he'd been clear-headed and not doped up he probably woulda killed you, raped your wife, and then killed her."

"Oh, my God," Ned proclaimed. "If we'd known that we'd just left the van and rode into town with that nice couple that told you about us being stranded up here."

"You're darn lucky they came along. Most folks have cleared out of the mountains by now. Hardly anybody drives up here this time of year. Just consider yourselves fortunate, but don't you be prowlin' around up here anymore. Keep that fancy van on the main roads or in town," Gil instructed firmly. "Y'all ride back to town in the tow truck. I'm headed up the mountain to see if I can catch up to the fugitive."

"You're not going to catch him up there," Ned informed.

"Why not?"

"He's not up there anymore. Long gone. Passed by here an hour or so before you got here. Almost ran into our van and darn near drove off the mountain right yonder where there aren't any boulders on the side along the road."

"Wish he had," Gil exclaimed. "Sorry folks, shouldn't 'a said that. Wasn't professional, but I've been chasin' this guy for a year and he's always one step ahead of me. He's got to be stopped one way or another before he hurts or kills someone else."

Ned and Lana climbed aboard the tow truck and accompanied the driver to the only tire shop in Leadville where they purchased two new tires before they headed to the High Country Café for the chicken fried steak dinner, known throughout the region as the best. After they consumed the delicious fare the couple drove to a small historic home they had rented for their time in the town. Leadville had always been their peaceful respite from the troubles and crimes of the "real" world where they lived. The couple trembled in fear as thoughts of a murdering rapist on the run in the area engulfed both their minds. Ned kept the fully loaded .22 caliber handgun close as they locked the doors and settled in for the evening.

Gil headed up the mountain to the spot where the couple had seen Herron and there he searched for any sign of the fugitive. He hoped that the rapist had accidently left some clue as to his destination, but he really had no inkling of discovery of any real hard evidence. As he walked through the head high native grasses along the winding stream Gil found numerous shell casings that he assumed came from Herron's erratic use of a firearm.

* * *

"That couple were real lucky folks," Gil noted. "If Herron had been clear-headed enough to realize they were there I have no doubt that he woulda raped the woman and killed them both. Far as I know it'd been a long dry spell for Herron. Hadn't raped anybody or killed anybody and I expect he was gettin' desperate to satisfy his evil desires."

"I thought he liked teenaged girls," Randy reminded.

"They were his preference. It had been nearly a year since he raped Marcia and to my knowledge that had been his last 'encounter'. Those magazines he stole from the Mine Shaft Bookstore weren't real explicit, but they were just racy enough to stir 'im up. Make 'im want the real thing."

"Maybe he found satisfaction with some 'working' girls," Randy suggested. "I've heard there's a bunch of 'em around these tourist towns. At one time, Leadville had more than its share of brothels."

"Not any more. Not in my county," Gil declared firmly. "We don't allow such goin's-on in Lake County. We don't want guys just lookin' for a good time. They can find it somewhere else, but not in my territory."

* * *

A heavy snow storm moved in as Gil drove the Land Cruiser down the treacherous road that stretched from the high tundra into Leadville. The blinding precipitation not only hindered the trip down the mountain, it also greatly discouraged the sheriff. He assumed that Herron had a remote cabin hideout somewhere way back in the mountains equipped and ready for the cold months ahead. Winter had been the fugitive's ally, but Gil's determination grew stronger. *It ain't gonna happen again*, Gil thought. *I will catch that bastard before winter immobilizes the area. I will catch 'im.*

When the sheriff arrived in an area known as Little Strayhorse Gulch, nature issued an urgent call. *Ah geez, I gotta pee*, he thought as he pulled to the side of the road. *Probably gonna freeze, but I just can't wait. If I don't relieve myself right now, the seat's gonna be all wet before I get to town. How would I explain that?* As he stood behind a tree and took care of nature's call Gil glanced down the road where an old tool shed had been converted into a cabin, decades earlier. The structure had been occupied by the infamous Baby Doe Tabor for the last thirty-five years of her life.

The sight of the old dilapidated cabin brought history of the area to Gil's mind as he peered at it while he continued taking care of "business." Baby Doe came to Leadville during the silver boom and married Horace Tabor, who had attained great wealth through his mining interests. He built the Tabor Grand Hotel which later became the Delaware, the same place where Gil Gentry lived. Ownership and operation of the Tabor Opera Houses in both Denver and Leadville added to his affluence. The Tabors enjoyed a life of opulence for many years, but after the bottom dropped out of the silver market they lived in poverty. Shortly before he died, Horace Tabor instructed Baby Doe that she should not sell the Matchless Mine since he assumed that a rebound in the silver market loomed in the future. The widow, who apparently suffered from some type of dementia, moved into the old tool shed at the Matchless Mine. The intriguing woman met her demise when she froze to death during a severe snow storm in the winter of 1935. Gil had developed a fascination for the history of the area, had researched extensively the Tabor story, and Leadville's many other colorful characters and tales. The man who had little interest in education as a youngster had become extremely well-read on the folklore of Leadville and Lake County.

As the sheriff completed the task at hand he observed smoke that ascended from the stove pipe atop the old shed. *That's real odd,* he thought. *Nobody's lived in that place since '35. Only folks that ever go in there are tourists and the tour guide, and that doesn't happen this late in the day. It'll be dark soon.* As the sheriff crept closer on foot he spotted a vehicle parked behind the structure, a white Chevy pickup. He quickly, but quietly retreated to the Toyota.

"Sheriff Gentry here. Get me some backup up here at the Matchless Mine," he instructed over the radio.

"What's happening?" the dispatcher questioned.

"I think I've got Herron cornered in Baby Doe's old shack. Tell 'em to move in real quiet-like, no flashing lights or sirens. Tell 'em to park down the road a piece and approach on foot. I'm parked just up the road a short distance and have an eyeball on the place. Don't want to spook 'im."

As darkness descended on the mountains Gil hoped that Herron had not spotted the Toyota where he sat and waited for backup. Unfortunately, strong winds had blown the clouds out, and the sheriff feared the bright glow of the moon that illuminated the landscape, reflected off the new fallen snow, shined on the Land Cruiser, and like a spotlight may have revealed his presence.

He noted no movement in the moonglow around the cabin as he waited nervously for the arrival of his deputies, but suddenly the pop of a gun emanated from the shed. The driver's side window of the Land Cruiser shattered, shards of glass flew over the sheriff, and as he heard a second shot, he felt the rush of air from a bullet that passed within an inch of his head. Herron had spotted Gil's vehicle. "Shots fired," he announced over the radio.

"Backup should be there any minute," came the response.

Multiple shots rang out and several bullets struck the Toyota with a thud. Gil crouched low as he exited the vehicle from the passenger side and stealthily moved in closer to the cabin with his Smith and Wesson drawn. Several more bullets whizzed through the air before the sheriff returned fire. A hail of lead filed the air as the firefight between the fugitive and the lawman intensified.

"Where the hell have you been?" Gil asked when several deputies arrived.

"You just couldn't wait 'til we got here?" one deputy questioned. "Started the party without us. Wanted all the fun for yourself."

"You guys work your way around the cabin and get it surrounded. Maybe we'll get lucky and kill the son-of-a-bitch."

Fortunately, none of the lawmen took a hit as the gunfire continued for nearly an hour before things finally went silent. "We've got the place surrounded. Come out with your hands in the air where I can see 'em," Gil instructed.

After the sheriff repeated the demand, still no response came from the cabin. "Maybe we've killed the bastard."

As the sheriff contemplated his team's next move a voice shouted from the inside the shed. "Don't shoot, I'm coming out." The door opened, and Herron emerged from the structure with his hands held high. Gil raised his gun, took dead aim at Herron's forehead, and for a brief-moment Gil thought, *One more shot could end this thing for good.*

"Don't do it, Gil," Deputy Long implored. "You'll regret it. You've got to live with yourself."

"Nah, bad as I'd like to I ain't gonna," Gil responded as he lowered his gun. "Let the system handle it."

Gil felt relief as he approached the murdering rapist, threw him to the ground with somewhat more than necessary force, and secured him with handcuffs. He placed the long-sought-after fugitive in one of the squad cars, and headed to town. The chase had ended.

* * *

"Sorry devil ruined the Toyota. It was riddled with bullets. Windows just about all busted, and headlights shattered. Radiator was spewin' fluid. Had to leave my favorite vehicle just sittin' there. Don't know what kept me from gettin' hit."

"Yeah, or the gas tank. If it had blown, it mighta killed you."

"For sure," Gil responded. "Just can't figure why I was able to walk away unscathed."

"Apparently the 'Big Guy' was watching out for you. How come Herron gave up?" Randy asked.

"Damn fool ran out of ammo," Gil answered.

"That was a stroke of luck."

"After what he did to Marcia, I sure wanted to shoot the S.O.B. right between the eyes, maybe shoot him someplace else first, like right between his legs, and then finish him off, but that would have been too easy on 'im. Just let 'im have some time to think about dyin' from the stick of the needle. I figured that was more punishment."

CHAPTER 13

THE JUROR

Drat it, Katy Edmond thought as she opened a letter from the Jury Commissioner of the Lake County Justice Center. *It's been a long time since I got a jury summons. Why now? That rape and murder trial is coming up and I sure don't want to be on that jury. Never been a big believer in the death penalty and I don't know if I could give him death, but if anybody deserves it, it's that creep.*

Katy had received jury summons in years past, but at that time her three young children required her constant attention and she received an exemption from service. The two boys now attended school and her older son looked out for the younger one after school until the mother's shift ended at the High Country Cafe. A trusted friend cared for Katy's youngest child, the toddler, Brenda. The mother realized that she probably no longer had an excuse acceptable to those in charge of jury selection and because of the small jury pool in Lake County her participation seemed imminent.

Since the loss of her husband, Rex, life had been difficult, but the resourceful woman worked hard and provided for her children. With no formal education beyond high school she accepted employment clerking in several local stores that only paid minimum. After her move to waitressing at the High Country Café, she soon learned that her cheerful personality brought in substantial tips and greatly increased her income that supplied provisions for her family.

* * *

Randy listened intently as Gil related his story, but Katy's thoughts returned to her roots in the Ozark Mountains of Arkansas where she first appeared on this earth. Large timber, high peaks, and lush valleys made up the picturesque landscape where the youngest of three sisters grew up in the small town of Green Forest. Distant memories from long ago conjured up visions of her childhood home that she left behind many years before. The tiny hamlet boasted a population of approximately seven-hundred-fifty souls in 1942, the year of her birth.

Involvement in church activities, school functions, and a close relationship with her mother's family dominated Katy's childhood. Few other entertainment or recreational activities existed in the rural area. Unlike Gil, who grew up without maternal influence, the girl lived in a home filled with the love and respect of her mother, but with the absence of her father. The admirable traits from her mother infiltrated Katy's personality.

Katy's young mind had blocked it out and she remembered little of the incidents that caused her father's expulsion from their home. She did remember the way he stared at her and her sisters, a look not consistent with fatherly love, but more a look of lust. When the mother caught the father involved in perverted actions with one of Katy's sisters it infuriated the woman and she sent him packing with the threat of arrest and prosecution if he ever returned. Katy never saw or heard from her father after that day.

Fiercely loyal, when Katy loved, she loved deeply and unconditionally. Before Gil there had been Katy's high school sweetheart, Rex. The two had known each other since their grade school days. They had lived only a short distance apart and had grown up together in a close relationship like that of a brother and sister. The two spent vast amounts of time with one another during their childhood, became a number in high school, and as expected by family and classmates, they married right after graduation. Their early marriage had been a struggle, but love and mutual respect had sustained them and had made their relationship strong. Rex sought a better life for his young bride and future children. Because of the almost nonexistent employment opportunities in the hills of Arkansas the concerned husband sought career prospects elsewhere.

* * *

"Katy, you still with us?" Gil questioned as he gazed adoringly at his wife. Gil had been the happy recipient of her admirable attributes for many years. Katy loved her late husband, Rex, wholeheartedly, but she worshiped her man, Gil Gentry, and he idolized his woman. Although now in her mid-sixties, in his mind's eye he saw the vivacious young woman he had married nearly thirty years earlier. Her thick, dark hair had thinned some and strands of gray that now mingled among her darker locks reminded Gil of the precious silver from mines in the area. To Katy's husband, regardless of graying hair or a few wrinkles here and there, her timeless beauty remained.

"Yeah, just kinda dozed off and was thinking about how I wound up here."

"I'm sure glad you did," Gil injected. "No tellin' what woulda become of me if you hadn't."

"I've wondered about that myself," Randy noted. "Not about what woulda become of you, Uncle Gil, but how Katy ended up in Leadville. I know you grew up in Arkansas, but I never knew how come you came to Colorado."

"There was bit of a parallel between Gil and my first husband."

* * *

Soon after high school graduation and before his marriage to Katy, Rex sought employment to support himself and his wife-to-be. The young man had no marketable job skills or educational background, so he accepted a job as a truck driver in the Arkansas poultry industry. As a driver for Tyson Foods for several years, he delivered truckloads of chicks to the hundreds of farmers who raised them for the company, and he hauled grown chickens from the farms to market. The job had no real future, it only offered a lifetime spent behind the wheel of a truck with minimal pay, and Rex wanted more. Like Gil, he had read about similar truck-driving possibilities at the Climax Mine near Leadville, but with greater compensation and future opportunities than offered by the Arkansas poultry industry. The young man had longed for a life beyond the hills of the Ozarks, so in 1967 he and Katy, who had become pregnant, packed up what few belongings they possessed and headed to the Rocky Mountains of Colorado.

The sleepy little town of Leadville, with a population totaling just over four thousand, seemed like a large city to the young couple from Green Forest, Arkansas, a town that had grown little by the year they left, when it reported a population of only twelve hundred. Although more majestic, the high mountain summits that towered to fourteen thousand feet and beyond, the many clear cold streams, and the vast valleys of the Rockies reminded the wife of her home in Arkansas except on a much grander scale.

* * *

"Wow. What a coincidence," Randy asserted. "You both worked in trucking, you drove logging trucks, Rex hauled chickens, and you both sought life beyond the horizon. The two of you wound up at the Climax. Sounds like two peas in a pod."

"Well, that's a stretch. There's a big distinction between logs and chickens," Gil noted with a chuckle. "But, I reckon there were some parallels."

"Somewhat, but there were some big differences, too," Katy responded. "Gil was almost thirteen years older than Rex. At the time, I would have considered him a real old man and wouldn't have given him a second thought. Gil is tall and although you wouldn't know it now, he was quite muscular, had a real trim waist, but real broad shoulders. Rex was lank, and his shoulders weren't wide at all and I reckon by comparison he was kinda puny. He was strong enough, but not like Gil."

"Hey, now. What do you mean 'you wouldn't know it now'?" Gil chided. "I'm still a perfect specimen of virile manhood."

"You'd best take a look in a mirror, old man. Your shoulders are still broad, if kinda slumped over, and what ever happened to that trim middle?" Katy replied with a giggle.

"Maybe so, but you still like me," Gil asserted with a gleam in his eye. "Besides, it's your cookin' that took away my slim waistline."

"Gil was unsettled, had itchy feet, as he liked to say. Even though Rex wanted life away from Green Forest, he had become settled here in Leadville. He liked it a lot and had no desire to move anywhere else. He liked his job at the Climax and he eventually got promoted to a supervisory position that paid better and offered more benefits than truck driving."

"I'll have to admit that he was more settled," Gil responded. "But he had you and the kids to keep him grounded. I didn't have nothin' until you and me got together."

"Ain't nothing like a good woman," Randy declared.

"You got that right. Katy is the best. I'm the luckiest guy on earth."

"Reckon I'd have to challenge that," Randy exclaimed. "I'm pretty darn lucky myself. Got the best around. Don't come any better than Barbara."

"I know that's right," Gil agreed. "We're both real lucky men. Don't know how our gals put up with the likes of us."

"It's not easy," Katy informed. "If Barb was here she would agree."

* * *

Rex and Katy enjoyed a good life in the mountains, he worked hard at his job, and she toiled diligently at home. Care of Brandon, their firstborn, and the daily household routine filled her days. A hot bath greeted the husband each night and a homecooked meal served in the spotless surroundings of their one-hundred-year-old house awaited him upon his return from the mine. Soon the pleasures of marriage produced a second son, Hunter, born in 1970. The couple made many friends in their new hometown, and although the lack of the close association with family back in Arkansas left a void for Katy, they considered things nearly perfect. The couple had settled into life in the idyllic town of Leadville and had become a part of the community. They had each other, two young children, a decent income, and a really nice home, so nothing else mattered.

The year 1977 brought both abundant joy and devastating sadness to Katy. *I'll cook Rex his favorite supper and make it a special evening for him. And when we go to bed I'll tell him the good news,* Katy thought as she left her doctor's office where she had just been informed of the expectation of a third child in time for Christmas. *What a wonderful Christmas present. I know Rex, he'll be thrilled. I love my boys, but I sure hope this one's a girl. Sure do wish Mom had lived long enough to have a granddaughter, but I reckon she knows.*

A screaming siren jolted Katy from her pleasant thoughts as she drove toward home with great care since a layer of fresh snow made the streets extremely slick. *Somebody probably skidded off the road somewhere out north of town. Hope nobody's hurt bad,* she thought as she pulled to the side of Harrison Avenue when a Sheriff's Department car and an ambulance approached with lights flashing, sirens blaring, and horns honking. *Sure hope everyone is okay.*

* * *

"And that's how we met for the first time," Gil informed.

"What are you talking about?" Randy questioned.

"It wasn't a car that had skidded off the road, but there had been an accident at the Climax and a phone call just would not do."

* * *

Katy scurried around, prepared a scrumptious meal, set the dining table with a white table cloth and her best tableware. She fed Brandon and Hunter early and sent them to their room. Although he did not know what, as the elder brother observed his mom when she placed candles and wine glasses on the table, he realized that she had good and important news of some kind for his father. At her request, the boy kept his younger brother occupied and out of the way.

When Katy heard sounds of a car that pulled into the driveway and the closing of its door she hurriedly crossed the room toward the door. She stopped and peered in a mirror that hung on a wall next to the entrance, ran her hands through her hair and fluffed it up, just the way Rex liked it. It appeared to the excited wife that her makeup had been properly applied so that it accentuated what her husband called her natural beauty. The excited wife looked her best as she anticipated the revelation of wonderful news to her husband. The expectant mother planned a warm embrace and a juicy kiss as she stood by the door and waited for the father's appearance.

Brandon knew something had gone horribly wrong when he heard his mother as she shrieked, "Oh, God no. Not Rex." As the boy entered the room he did not see his father as expected, but instead a big tall man that wore a sheriff's uniform stood at the door. Katy slumped onto the sofa and sobbed in uncontrollable anguish.

"I'm real sorry, Mrs. Edmond," Gil Gentry affirmed compassionately. "The best I can tell you is, he did not suffer. Probably never knew what happened. It was a real freak accident. According to witnesses he was headed toward the mine entrance and a boulder just busted loose, rolled down the incline above the entrance and rolled right over 'im. Killed 'im instantly."

"What's happening?" Brandon asked as he ran to his mother.

"It's your father," she cried as she pulled the boy close. "There was an accident at the mine . . .oh, God. He's dead."

Hunter knew his mother and brother experienced great sadness, but he understood little of what had happened. Katy gathered both her sons into her arms and sobbed soulfully.

Slow mournful music played softly in the background as Katy gazed upon her husband who lay in repose at the Hailey-Fenton Funeral Home. "I don't mean any disrespect," she assured, "but, turn off that sad music. Rex was not a sad guy. He was full of life and enjoyed every minute he walked this earth. Play something lively and cheerful or nothing at all."

The request seemed a little unusual to the funeral director as most folks paid little attention to that detail. "Yes, ma'am," he replied as he rummaged through his collection of tapes in search of just the right one. He came across a tape that he did not considerate appropriate for a funeral, one he had put together for a different type of event. It included the Shaun Cassidy rendition of *Da Doo Ron Ron, Gonna Fly Now* by Bill Conti, The Eagles performance of

Hotel California, It Was Almost Like a Song sung by Ronnie Milsap, and several other upbeat offerings.

"Just don't seem right to me, Mrs. Edmond," he declared.

"That tape is perfect. It says, 'I am Rex, remember me for loving life,'" Katy responded. "At the funeral, I want *I'll Fly Away* sung as the final song. That was his favorite gospel song and it expresses his faith of another life beyond the clouds."

"As you wish."

Many friends and townspeople surrounded Katy as the minister spoke words of faith and comfort and those closest to Rex told stories of their relationships with the deceased, both serious and humorous. Brandon and Hunter stood by their mother's side as they laid her beloved husband to rest in the Evergreen Cemetery. Katy's life was forever changed.

* * *

"Gads, what a horrible thing to happen," Randy gasped.

"Yes, it was," Katy replied. "I thought my life was over. There I was, a widow at thirty-five with two young children and another one on the way. To say I was devastated and depressed is an understatement."

"How on earth did you handle it? I'm a little surprised you didn't go back home to Arkansas."

"I thought about it, but Mom was gone to her glory by then and my sisters were scattered so there wasn't really anything to go home to. I grieved deeply and had it not been for my faith and the help of good friends I don't know what I would have done. After a while I realized that I had to take care of the kids and try to make a happy life for them. I knew that's what Rex would have wanted me to do."

* * *

Although different than when Rex enriched her existence, a certain normalcy returned to the young widow's life. Her children's well-being and happiness became the main focus of Katy's efforts. She worked several different jobs until she finally landed at the High Country Café. With income from the café along with social security benefits for her minor dependents, the mother managed a decent living for her kids and herself. The routine she had developed came crashing down when her selection as a juror on the Richard Herron trial interrupted her life.

* * *

"I really thought I wouldn't get picked. The jury pool in Lake County was larger than I expected, but still small by big city standards. I thought surely out of all those people they'd leave me alone," Katy noted.

"Looks like your feelings about the death penalty woulda disqualified you," Randy assumed.

"Trouble is when they asked me about it, I had to tell the truth. I had real reservations about capital punishment, but after what Herron did and if they proved his guilt beyond any reasonable doubt then I knew I could agree to give him death and I told 'em so."

"But what about the kids, who would look after them if you were sequestered?"

"Thankfully, they didn't sequester the jury. The judge gave us a stern warning that we were not to read or watch any news about the trial and he threatened us with contempt of court and jail time if we discussed the case with anyone. He didn't have to tell me but once. I wasn't about to break the rules and maybe go to jail. I kept the TV turned off, didn't open the newspaper, and kept my mouth shut. Life for the kids went on pretty much as usual. Brandon looked after Hunter after school until I got home."

"But what about Brenda?" Randy questioned.

"Baby Brenda was born in December of 1977, eight months after Rex's death. When the trial commenced, she was almost three, too young for Brandon to care for, so she spent her days with a sitter who was a close friend that I trusted completely."

"Sounds like you had all the bases covered."

"I did my best, but what I hadn't figured on was the nightmares."

With her selection to the jury on the high-profile murder case, Katy's life had taken on a dimension unlike anything she had ever known or thought of in her wildest imagination.

CHAPTER 14

THE SELECTION

WHAT SHOULD I WEAR? KATY THOUGHT AS SHE SEARCHED through the clothes that hung in her small closet. She selected one dress after another and held them in front of her as she looked in the full-length mirror that stood in one corner of her bedroom. A black ensemble she normally wore to funerals did not appear appropriate, while her favorite outfit of red that she seldom wore seemed a bit too much. *Don't want to look too flashy, but that's not a problem, I'm not a flashy gal, but I don't want to look dowdy. I want to look nice, but not like "come on, pick me." I sure do not want to get picked.* The confused woman finally settled on a dressy dark navy-blue outfit that did not appear either elaborate, or plain. Katy wore the conservative dress to many church functions and she thought of it with amusement as her "church lady" costume. Her long brunette hair normally cascaded down over her shoulders in curly locks, but as the completion of her planned look for the current occasion, Katy pulled it straight back and formed a bun at the nape of her neck. The cunning lady applied minimal makeup as she looked in the mirror. The devious young woman removed the contact lenses that she usually wore and replaced them with heavy dark rimmed glasses. *There, that's the look I'm going for,* Katy thought as she giggled nervously when she saw her reflection in the glass. *If I look like a "church lady," surely, they'll rule me out.*

I've never seen this lot so full of cars, Katy thought as she pulled into the parking lot at the courthouse on Harrison Avenue. Panic set in as she drove up and down through the rows of cars that filled all the spaces. *Don't want to draw attention to myself coming in late. If I don't find a parking place real quick, that's what's gonna happen.* Katy spotted a car that backed out of a place near the street. Just as she circled around one row of parked cars, drove hurriedly toward the empty space, another vehicle approached from the opposite direction, cut in front of her, and turned into the only available spot on the lot. *Oh, darn. Now what?* She thought as she lay down on her horn. The occupant of the offending car emerged from the vehicle and never looked in Katy's direction as he calmly walked toward the courthouse steps. *Is this how my day is gonna be? I'm late, can't find a parking place, and I'll probably get picked for God knows what kinda trial. Maybe it'll be some kinda civil case. Just as long as I don't get put on the juror for that rape and murder trial.*

As the distraught woman pulled out of the parking lot onto Harrison Ave she observed one empty spot on the opposite side of the street from where the courthouse stood. This time her luck held out as she made a quick U-turn and secured the space. The tardy member of the jury pool virtually ran across the street, sprinted across the parking lot, up the steps, through the door, and bounded up the stairs to the second floor. As she entered the room where the jury pool congregated the commissioner greeted her sarcastically from the bench. "So glad you could join us, young lady. Now take a seat so we can get this show started."

Katy let out a sigh of relief as she sat down and looked around at the jury pool much larger than she had anticipated. She figured with the number of people gathered as potential jurors the odds of her selection had been minimized, especially for the high-profile rape and murder case. The mostly uptight potential jurors squirmed and shifted in their seats, but they settled down and sat quietly when the normal routine started. Many folks approached the bench with one excuse or another. The commissioner relieved some of their duty, but ordered others back to their seats. It seemed to Katy that the process took forever, but that did not matter so long as she did not get chosen.

Her turn finally came, and she approached the bench. "I'm a single parent with three young children."

"Who is caring for the kids today?" the commissioner questioned.

"The two older ones are in school and the toddler is with a good friend."

"Do you have a job?"

"Yes, sir."

"Who watches them after school while you're at work?"

"Uh, the older boy watches the younger one and the friend watches the baby," Katy answered.

"So, you have arrangements for their care regardless if you're on a jury or at work."

"Yes, sir," she replied sheepishly as she figured her fate had been sealed.

"Return to you seat, young lady. You are not excused."

"You trying to get picked," a gentleman who sat next to Katy whispered.

"You're the guy that stole my parking place."

"Was that you? I'm real sorry about that. Hope you will forgive me," he replied guiltily. "I didn't want to be late. As you've probably figured out, the commissioner doesn't like folks to be late. I had no idea there was a woman driving that car. I promise, had I known I would not have taken the space."

From the man's contrite tone Katy felt that the apology had been heartfelt and sincere, so she graciously accepted it. "What did you mean was I trying to get picked?"

"You're dressed for the part," the man in sloppy attire replied.

"I've been here a bunch of times and it didn't take me long to learn that how you dress has a bearing on getting picked or not."

"What do you mean?"

"They like folks dressed neat and conservative just like you are. You'd been better off looking kinda frowsy and dumb, or even flashy, you know, kinda like a floozy. You look studious, intelligent, and professional, you know, like a lawyer or judge or maybe a librarian. That's what they want. You'll get picked. I'd bet on it."

"You two got something you want to share?" the commissioner asked with irritation. Or can we proceed?"

* * *

"Katy, I didn't figure you had a devious bone in your body!" Randy claimed. "Dressing in a way that you thought would keep you from getting picked. I can't believe it. Straight arrow Katy. You've destroyed my illusions."

"When it came to me getting picked for jury duty or not, I thought, 'whatever it takes'. I was scared to death I'd get selected for the rape and murder trial."

"Katy soon found out that the manner of dress had no bearing on who got picked," Gil informed.

"According to the guy sitting next to me, it did make a diffcrence and I had got it all backwards. Apparently, it didn't matter since he got chosen too."

"It might have had some real tiny effect, but I think it is more in a person's attitude and how they answer questions," Gil suggested. "And I think Katy found that out."

"Randy, you should have seen the jury selection process," Katy declared. "It was like the defense lawyer was already working his case."

* * *

Sure do wish they'd get this over with so I can get out of here and go to work, Katy thought as the preliminary process continued. Her mind concentrated on other things rather than the current situation. She just wanted out of there. *I'll have to go home and change clothes, but if this doesn't take too long maybe I can get to the High Country before the lunch rush. That's when I get the best tips.* By the time the commissioner had listened to all the excuses put forth by those who wanted a suspension of their service, the noon hour had arrived. The stern-faced man called a recess for lunch, but he seriously warned the prospective jurors of severe consequences should they not return or if they arrived late.

Katy knew from the response to her late arrival that morning any further tardiness would not go unnoticed by the commissioner. Even though she had no real interest in food at that point, the smartly dressed woman decided on the Golden Burro Café and Lounge. Katy realized parking places were at a premium near the courthouse, so she walked the several blocks to the café. Numerous potential jurors made the same choice and by chance she shared a table with several of them including Larry, the man who had stolen her parking place, but had warned her about her mode of dress. The prospective jurors exchanged pleasantries while they ate. They engaged in conversation about the selection process, their families, and their jobs. The group consisted of folks from all walks of life and some hoped for exclusion, while others desired service.

"Oh, great!" Katy shrieked when she suddenly realized that time had slipped away while the group engaged in chit-chat. "We'd better make a mad dash back to the courthouse. We are already late."

"Glad you folks decided to grace us with your presence. Aren't you the young lady that came in late this morning?" the commissioner asked as he starred at Katy when the group entered the room. "I was fixin' to send the sheriff after you. The six of you report to courtroom three."

* * *

"I know darn well being late is part of what landed us in that particular courtroom," Katy espoused.

"I'm glad I didn't have to come get you" Gil stated with a chuckle. "But, then I woulda renewed our acquaintance sooner."

"Oh, yeah. I can see it now," Katy commented. "Probably woulda come on to me while you locked me up."

"Probably. A good-lookin' gal like you, why not?" Gil retorted as he shot a loving smile at his wife. "You woulda given my old drab jail some sparkle and a touch of class."

"You two are just too weird," Randy quipped. "Do you really think being late made a difference?"

"Yes, I do," Katy answered.

"Nope! It didn't. The courtroom assignments had already been made," Gil added.

"Gil doesn't know what he's talking about, Randy. Seems like a real coincidence that all six of us that were late got sent to same horrendous trial."

* * *

"Tell 'em you're unemployed and can't find a job," Larry advised as they sat on the back row of the courtroom. "They don't like folks that can't find a job."

"I can't do that," Katy replied. "That'd be a lie and I can't lie. Besides, I don't think that's true anyway."

"You watch," he quipped. "If they question me that's what I'm gonna tell 'em and I bet I get off."

Much to their chagrin, Katy, Larry, and the other prospective panelists soon learned that they had been selected as potential jurors for the rape and murder trial of Richard Herron. The process dragged on for what seemed like hours as the throng of humanity awaited their fate. Would they be chosen as jurors for the high-profile case or would they go home? Before the questioning process began the bailiff escorted a nice looking, well-dressed, clean shaven young man with short neatly styled hair to the defense table.

"Is that the defendant?" Katy questioned in a whisper as she leaned toward Larry.

"That'd be him," he answered. "Boy, they really cleaned him up good for the trial. From what I heard he had long greasy hair and a full beard. They're trying to make a good impression on whoever gets picked for the jury."

The interrogation of prospective jurors seemed endless as the prosecutor, the defense lawyer, and the judge asked many questions. Some appeared trivial and totally unrelated to the case and looked as if they had no bearing on the process at hand. The elimination of one person after the other took place either at the objection of the prosecution or the defense. Katy breathed easy as the procedure continued since it appeared that the pickiness of both sides might expedite her rejection.

Ten jurors had been selected when they called Larry to the stand. He stated his name on request and informed that unemployment plagued him and after several minutes of questioning the judged declared, "hearing no objection from either side, you are hereby remanded to duty. Take a seat in the juror box. Next up, please, and state your name."

"Kathleen Edmond, but everyone knows me as Katy."

"Occupation."

"Waitress at the High Country Café."

"Oh, yeah. I've seen you there. Best chicken fried steak in

Colorado." The judge's attitude had lightened up and Katy felt her exclusion from service had probably been secured. "You seem like a sensible young woman. Let me ask you about capital punishment. What is your attitude regarding the death penalty?"

"I've never much believed in it, unless charges are proven one-hundred percent with absolutely no doubt of a defendant's guilt of some really heinous crime."

The prosecutor asked a deluge of questions before the defense had its turn.

"Would you send a nice young man like this to death row?" he asked as he pointed to Richard Herron who sat at the defendant's table.

"Like I said, it depends on the charges and if they are proven without doubt," Katy responded.

"The defense objects to this juror, your honor."

"Before I decide to dismiss you or not, I have one more question Mrs. Edmond."

"Yes, your honor."

"Do you see anything wrong with our judicial system?"

"Yes, sir, I do."

"And what would that be?" the judge asked with surprise.

"No disrespect, your honor, but you bleeding-heart liberal judges turn scumbags loose to commit more atrocities. If proven guilty, at the very least they should be locked up for life if not given death." The response shocked folks in the courtroom and it even surprised Katy that she spoke out so boldly. She later learned that the man was known as the hanging judge of Lake County and her response pleased him greatly.

"Get her out of here," the defense lawyer insisted.

"Take a seat in the jury box, Mrs. Edmond. I like your audacity."

"Objection, your honor," defense shouted.

"Objection overruled. We have our jury. Everyone else is dismissed."

"What happened, Larry?" Katy whispered. "Your unemployed thing didn't work out too well."

"No, but I reckon I was right about the way you're dressed."

"Ladies and gentlemen of the jury, listen closely, hear, and heed my admonitions. Due to the nature of the alleged offenses against the defendant I would prefer that you be sequestered for the duration of this trial." *Oh, no. I can't be sequestered. I didn't expect such a thing and I haven't made any arrangements for the kids.* "However, there are no suitable accommodations in the city of Leadville for said sequester. Therefore, you will be free to return to your homes each evening, but you are not to listen to any news on radio, watch any TV newscast, or read newspaper articles about the case. You are not to discuss the case or any aspect of the trial with anyone. Any juror found to be in violation of any of the above will be held in contempt. Folks, this is a most serious case with multiple charges. A man's life is in your hands and I will not tolerate any infraction that might result in a mistrial. Go home. Enjoy your evening, but remember and adhere to these admonitions. We will see you at 9:00 in the morning. Do not be late."

* * *

"It seemed to me that the judge looked straight at me when he told us not to be late. I thought my worst nightmare had come to pass, but it had only just started," Katy asserted. "I did not want to be on that jury."

"Yeah, but the trial is what brought us together," Gil reminded.

"If we were meant to be together and apparently, we were, we would have met again anyway. I could have been spared the nightmares, and emotional anxiety heaped on me by that trial. It was the most ungodly thing I've ever experienced."

"Did the other four that came in late with you and Larry get chosen?" Randy asked.

"No, just me and Larry."

"That proves my point," Gil asserted. "If being late had any bearing on selection, all six of you would have been chosen."

"The other four got lucky," Katy noted. "They did not have to live through the nightmare."

* * *

Katy's long nightmare, and the beginning of a new life had begun.

CHAPTER 15

THE DEFENDANT

"What do you think made Herron so crazy? Randy questioned. "I mean, he had to be a madman to do the things he did to Marcia."

"You've got that right. He was a total nut case, a complete psychopathic maniac. He obviously didn't have a conscience or any sense of right and wrong," Gil answered.

"Yeah, but what made him that way?"

"I don't reckon we'll ever really know, but we did learn a lot about his background durin' the investigation. He came from a troubled past that apparently started with his birth and home life growin' up."

"I think that's a copout," Randy asserted. "I've known a lot of people who were raised in less than perfect homes, but they didn't go out and rape and murder anyone. One of my closest friends was born unwanted and was abused by his father and a lot of other folks and he is one of the best men I know."

"Randy's right," Katy agreed. "Just look at you, Gil. Your upbringing sure wasn't that good and you're the best."

"Thanks, Darlin', but I guess things affect people differently," Gil replied. "But, no matter what kind of raisin' a person's had, it ain't no excuse to do the things that Herron did."

* * *

On an ungodly hot August day in 1954 the reading topped out at one hundred sixteen degrees on the Coca-Cola thermometer that hung in the shade at the Texaco station located on the only highway that ran through El Centro, California. The mountains around the town near the U.S. border with Mexico appeared as gigantic rock piles and they reflected the stifling desert heat. To most folks, it seemed much hotter than the official number. The intensity of the fiery atmosphere felt more like the flames of hell to Modeen Herron as she sat in front of an oscillating fan that did little more than stir up the hot air. The blazing sun burned her skin when the miserable woman left the confines of her house in search of relief by means of the almost nonexistent breezes outside. The expectant mother had reached the ninth month of her pregnancy and the unbearable heat exacerbated her condition.

"What the hell's wrong with you, woman?" The unfeeling Richard Herron Sr. asked when he heard his wife's moans.

"It's this ungodly heat," she answered. "It's just about to kill me. Why can't we move some place that ain't so damn hot?"

"Ain't no hotter than normal for this time of year. You think you'd be used to it."

"Well, being nine months pregnant don't make it any cooler."

"Woman, I'm gettin' damn tired of your complainin'. This is the fourth time you've been through this and all you do is bitch and complain ever' time. 'It's the heat. My belly hurts. My back aches. I'm about to pee my pants.' Bitch, bitch, bitch. That's all I ever hear out of you."

"Well, hell. That's the thanks I get for keepin' you happy. After this 'un's born maybe there just won't be no more 'happy' times."

"Don't matter none to me. Happiness is where you find it and I reckon I could find it someplace else. You'd best keep your damn mouth shut and keep on takin' care o' me or you'll find yourself out on the street. Now, when are you gonna get up off your lazy butt and fix my supper?"

"I'll get it started right away," the browbeaten wife responded sheepishly as she arose from the chair and left the minimal comfort offered by the fan.

When the miserable woman headed to the kitchen she let out a deafening shriek as she doubled over in pain, and water covered the floor at her feet. "My God, woman, look what a damn mess you done made."

"Richard, my water done broke and I been suffering from contractions for some time now. You'd best fire up the old Plymouth and take me to City Hospital."

"Can't it wait 'til after supper?"

"No, it can't. Now help me to the car."

Richard Herron Jr. entered a troubled life on August 15, 1954.

* * *

"Well, apparently, he was his father's son," Randy asserted. "Sounds like his old man was a real piece of work. Seems like I remember you telling me that he shared hardcore porn magazines with Jr. What kinda father does that?"

"The low life, scumbag kind," Gil replied.

"That's exactly what he was," Katy injected. "Rotten to the core. The defense tried to blame Herron's crimes on his upbringing during the trial."

"I kind'a think the ungodly heat on the day he was born was a sign that his life was gonna be hell and he'd heap the fires of Hades on everybody around him," Gil commented.

"Going all philosophical are you, Uncle Gil?" Randy asked.

"Just what I think. Just the ramblin's of a old lawman."

"Well, I think he was the devil hisself," Katy declared. "Came from the depths of hell and spread his evil everywhere. His lawyer also tried to blame his actions on severe migraines, but we didn't buy that one either. A doctor testified that he suffered from the debilitating headaches caused by an injury when Herron's father hit him in the head and knocked him unconscious."

"Good grief!" Randy exclaimed.

"From what we learned durin' the investigation he grew up in a hell of sorts," Gil responded.

* * *

Richard Sr. and Modeen Herron had been married slightly less than five years when Richard Jr. appeared as the youngest of four boys born to the couple. The large baby weighed in at nine pounds, three ounces and stretched out to nineteen and three-quarter inches. The mother barely recovered from each birth before she submitted to demands made by the obsessive husband. The burden and care of two toddlers and two babies still in diapers fell exclusively to the bedraggled mother. The uncaring father only considered the offspring as unfortunate accidents of his personal pleasures and nothing more. Gary, Martin, Mitchell, and Richard grew up in a home filled with tension, defined by abuse, and devoid of affection or love.

Young Richard never heard a kind or gentle word from his father and his mother had little time for any display of affection. The days of her life dragged by as she nursed the baby, fed the other boys, changed and washed diapers. One wretched incident taught the woman that the preparation of meals for her husband and the satisfaction of his obsessive physical demands took priority over her motherly duties.

"Where the hell is my supper?" Richard shouted as he observed an empty kitchen table when he returned home from a day of work as a garbage collector for the city El Centro.

"Ain't had time. The baby's been sick 'n throwin' up all afternoon," Modeen answered as she held baby Richard and wiped vomit residue from his face.

"To hell with that damn urchin," the husband screamed as he grabbed the baby from the mother's arms and literally threw him across the room where he landed in the crib. The highly agitated man turned around, glared at the wife, and backhanded the frightened woman repeatedly. "Now get your lazy ass to the kitchen and fix my supper."

Each time the baby screamed and Modeen headed toward the crib, Richard backhanded her and demanded his supper. The downtrodden wife wiped blood from her busted nose with one hand and prepared the meal for her malicious husband with the other. After she placed a plate of food in front of the man, the mother went to her baby.

"Get the hell back in here," Herron shouted. "You know I don't like to eat by myself."

"I ain't hungry," Modeen replied. "I got to see after the baby."

"You do what you're told, woman," he demanded as he arose from the table and stormed across the house to where Modeen held Richard Jr. He snatched the baby from her arms, threw him back in the crib, grabbed the mother by the shoulders, and dragged her back to the kitchen. "Now eat your supper," he screamed as he shoved his wife's face into a pot of piping hot beans that he took from the stove and sat on the table in front her.

After the despicable man finished his meal, he made other demands. The submissive wife complied, and the baby cried.

* * *

"Good God! What a miserable bastard," Randy declared. "Excuse my language, Katy. There are no words bad enough to describe him."

"It's okay," Katy responded. "You're right, there are no words."

"And it seems that's the way it went for Herron's entire childhood," Gil contended.

"I don't understand why any woman would stay with a guy like that and keep having his babies," Randy asserted.

"I've seen a lot of cases like that durin' my years as sheriff," Gil responded. "Seems like the women didn't have any regard for themselves and didn't think they could do any better. It is a sad indictment of our society, but it goes on all the time. And apparently that's how things went for Herron's entire life."

"The jury wasn't privy to some things in his background, but apparently Marcia wasn't his first victim," Katy noted.

* * *

As Richard Herron Jr. grew from a baby to a toddler, a young child, and a teenager he constantly witnessed the abuse of his mother by his father. Many times, the child and his siblings became victims of the attacks when Herron backhanded them or beat the crap out of them for some small or perceived offense. Pornographic magazines lay strewn about the house and the boys viewed the explicit smut with no admonition from their father or their mother. The actions of the son as he reached his mid-teens revealed that he had inherited his father's bad behaviors.

Many girls in El Centro High School found the tall, muscular Richard Herron an attractive, sexy specimen of manhood and he looked upon them as objects for pursuit and gratification of his lustful desires. Numerous female classmates succumbed to his demands, and after they satisfied his cravings, he tossed them aside like so much garbage. Lorena, a girl raised in a household of strict moral teaching, caught his eye and the pursuit commenced. It appeared to those closest to Herron that her conservative, almost dowdy manner of dress excited Herron. He voiced his curiosity as to what she hid under her long skirts and high-necked blouses. Her stellar character presented a challenge to Herron since he considered himself God's gift to the girls, and none of them in their right mind could resist what he offered. Lorena knew his reputation, she wanted no part of him, and she shunned his advances.

"Why does a looker like you dress like that?" Herron asked as he brushed up against Lorena in a lewd manner when he approached her in the hallway at school. "Bet you're hiding something real special under that drab outfit."

Lorena ignored him, walked briskly away, but when he caught up to her the scoundrel grabbed her by the shoulders, whirled her around, pulled her close, and kissed the surprised girl in front many of their classmates. *Whap,* the sound of hand to face echoed through the hall as Lorena landed a solid slap to Herron's cheek. The confrontation just excited and egged the rejected boy on to further onslaughts. When the final bell rang that ended the school day, Herron followed Lorena to the student parking lot where he accosted her once again.

"No slut turns me down," Herron shouted as he grabbed the object of his pursuit and dragged her into his old truck. "We're going out to a spot I know out in the mountains and you're gonna make me happy."

"I don't think so," Lorena shouted as a surge of energy raced through her body, she whopped Herron with her purse, and escaped through the passenger side door of the truck. Several friends ran to her aid when she screamed at the top of her lungs. Herron left them in a shower of gravel as he gunned the vehicle and sped away.

* * *

"We discovered several similar incidents durin' the investigation," Gil added.

"If I'd known about that part of his past, I wouldn't have hesitated to assess the death penalty," Katy asserted. "He obviously was no good to anybody and definitely a threat to society."

"Didn't they do anything about him?" Randy questioned.

"Lorena's parents filed a complaint, but later dropped it," Gil answered. "From what we were told by folks who knew the Herron family, Richard Sr. threatened her parents and they backed off. We did find a couple of cases where charges were filed, but the liberal California courts only gave him a slap on the wrist."

"What a travesty of justice," Randy noted. "If they'd done something back then, Marcia Leggett might still be alive."

"One lucky woman who succumbed to the no-good S.O.B. got smart after only a short time, and got away from him," Gil informed.

* * *

I can't believe a hunk like that would have migraines, Angie thought as she handed Herron a prescription usually prescribed for the debilitating headaches. The vivacious seventeen-year-old worked part-time at City Drugs, the only pharmacy in El Centro. The tall, muscular dark-haired young man caught her eye as he purchased the drug. A mutual attraction ensued when the customer detected the gleam in the clerk's beautiful eyes as she completed the transaction.

"You have migraines?" she asked.

"Yeah, I do. Pains me something awful, sometimes it's so bad that it puts me plumb out of commission for days," he replied. He realized that his condition garnered sympathy from the pretty blue-eyed blonde behind the counter, so he assumed the role as victim.

"Anybody ever figure out what causes 'em?"

"Head injury."

"You poor thing. What happened?"

"My old man hit me in the head when I was little. He hit me real hard. Knocked me unconscious. Wasn't the first time and sure wasn't the last."

"That's terrible," she sympathized.

"Ain't nothing compared to the beatings he gives me," he responded in his best "I'm a victim" voice. "He beats up on me and my brothers darn near ever day. Mom stays all bruised up where he hits her."

"Why does she stay with him?"

"Where's a woman with four kids gonna go?" he answered without revealing that his three brothers had grown to adulthood, left home, and escaped the abusive situation.

Richard Herron had tried every line in the book in his conquest of girls, but he had never played the victim card before. This one just came naturally as the girl showered him with pity and empathy when he wiped crocodile tears from his face. "It's every day's business," he sobbed. "He just beats the crap out of me for no good reason."

This is working real good, he thought as the shapely girl dressed in tight jeans and low-cut blouse came from behind the counter, put her arms around the "victim," and pulled him close. *Didn't know being a victim could be such a turn-on to girls.*

Over the next few weeks, the scoundrel played the role to perfection and Angie fell for it hook, line, and sinker. An intimate relationship immediately developed between the two; Herron packed up his things at his parents' home, and moved in with the unsuspecting girl. In April of 1979 the couple stood before a judge who looked at the couple with a disapproving eye when he observed Angie, whose midsection attested to the extent of their relationship. She professed her undying love for Richard, and he reluctantly said, "I do."

After only a few days, the groom who had been trapped by his own lusts lashed out at the bride. "You done got yourself pregnant on purpose just to get yourself a husband."

"I didn't do it by myself," she retorted. "You had a part in it."

"Don't talk to me like that, you bitch. You were supposed to take care of those things," he shouted. "You're just like my mother. She didn't take care o' things like a woman's supposed to and she ended up with a house full of brats." *Whap, whap.* The sound of the back of his hand as it struck her face echoed through the room. Suddenly, the "victim" became the perpetrator. Richard Herron Jr. had become just like his father and the fights escalated daily until Angie had had enough.

"Where the hell do you think you're going?" Herron asked as Angie packed her bags before she headed out the door into the heat from the hot July sun.

"I'm leaving," she answered.

"The hell you are. You ain't going no place," the irate husband screamed as he chased after the fed-up wife, grabbed her by the shoulders, whirled her around, and shook her like a rag doll. "Nobody walks out on Richard Herron. I'll let you know when I'm done with you. Now get your butt back in the house."

"I've had it and I ain't taking it from you no more. Get that through your thick skull. I'm done," the abused wife shouted as she pulled away from the abuser.

"Oh, you'll be back. Nobody else'll have you in your condition. You're damaged goods. Guys don't buy secondhand merchandise."

"That's the problem. You think I belong to you. Well, let me tell you, Mister, I ain't nobody's merchandise and I ain't for sale."

The pregnant woman became dizzy and nearly fainted numerous times as she struggled in the ungodly heat as she headed down the street toward the El Centro Greyhound Bus terminal. She purchased a ticket and boarded a bus bound for Eugene, Oregon. When Angie ran away from her family and hometown a year earlier she swore she had laid eyes on the city in the Northwest for the last time. Circumstances had changed dramatically, and she returned to the safe haven of her parents' home.

* * *

"Did Herron ever see her again?" Randy asked.

"Nope. He had no idea where she had gone since she had never spoken of her home," Gil answered. "He didn't even try to find her. She was just another conquest and he was done with her. Besides, she was pregnant, and he had no desire to be saddled with a kid."

"How do you know about her?"

"She saw an article about the rape and murder that named Richard as the defendant. She contacted my office and offered any testimony that might help seal his fate."

"What did he do after she left?"

"He promptly went back in the house and took a bunch of pills, I mean a bunch."

"You saying he tried to kill himself?"

"Yep, or so it appeared, but it didn't work out that way. Richard Sr. just happened by and called for help."

"That's hair bit surprising," Randy noted. "As rotten as he was you'd a thought he would' a just let 'im die."

"You'd think so," Gil responded. "But, unfortunately for Marcia Leggett he summoned help. That was in July and by September he had decided on Leadville as his new home."

* * *

Good riddance to that slut and her bastard kid, Herron thought as he contemplated his move. *I'll move someplace where nobody knows me, and I'll have me a real good time with ever' sweet young thing that comes along. If they tell me no, they will regret it. I'll take what I want before I give 'em what they deserve for rejecting me.*

CHAPTER 16

THE TRIAL

THE RICHARD HERRON CASE WEIGHED HEAVILY ON SHERIFF GIL Gentry's mind from the day of the crime until justice came to pass thirty years later. After a long wait of approximately one and one-half years since the villain allegedly raped and murdered Marcia Leggett at an isolated spot near Turquoise Lake, the trial finally commenced. At least folks thought so.

Katy Edmond had hoped that the expected cold front, with a forecast of heavy snow, had fizzled out when the sun peeked through a mountain pass to the east. However, much to her chagrin, cold north winds whistled through aspen and pine on the frosty March day in 1981. The raw conditions chilled her as she got the two older kids off to school before she dropped Brenda off at the trusted babysitter's. The inclement weather added stress to the task at hand as the juror hurriedly drove to the Lake County Courthouse. Katy arrived early and secured a parking place near the front door. The unhappy woman brushed snow from her hair and coat as she entered the building. Unfortunately, the norther had moved in as forecast, and it added to the disagreeableness of the day. Katy took no pleasure in her position as juror on the high-profile rape and murder case. She knew that her early arrival each morning kept her out of trouble with the judge. The reluctant juror had vowed that a repeat of her earlier transgressions during the jury selection would happen no more.

Other jurors meandered into the jury room as Katy waited nervously for the bailiff's escort into the court room. The panel fidgeted in their seats and talked among themselves, but Katy carefully avoided any discussion of the case at hand as they waited. The jurors wondered what had happened when the appointed time came and went with no word from the bailiff.

"Don't you think we should burn the scum?" A juror asked Katy.

"You'd best be quiet," she admonished. "Remember the judge's instructions."

"He ain't gonna know what we talk about."

"Just be quiet. I've got kids at home and don't have time to go to jail. Now be quiet," Katy commanded.

"You'd better listen to her," another juror chimed in. "This is serious business and the judge is one stern dude."

The inappropriate conversation ended when the judge summoned the group to the courtroom. They learned that the magistrate had denied a petition for a change of venue filed by the public defender, Mike Colton. The trial had been delayed pending an appeal of the ruling.

* * *

"That one guy was bound and determined to talk about the case. Kept saying we could go ahead and make a decision, since Herron was guilty as sin and ever'body knew it, but me and several of the others pretty much shut him down. I was real upset that the trial got delayed," Katy revealed. "I didn't want to be there. I just wanted to get the whole thing over and done with."

"How long was the delay?" Randy questioned.

"A little over two months. Two real long months. I was pretty much a prisoner in my own house during that time."

"What do you mean, a prisoner?"

"Had to stay close. Waiting on the phone call that would summon me back to the courthouse."

* * *

The much-awaited call finally came on the first Monday in June of 1981. The jurors received little advance notice, since the reconvening took place the next day. At least the wait had ended for Katy and the others. They dreaded the prolonged trial, but looked forward to its conclusion and their return to normal lives. It did not happen that way, as another delay ensued.

It seemed to Katy that history had repeated itself as she arose early, got the older kids off to school, and dropped Brenda off at the trusted friend's. Winter weather had mostly ended, but cool breezes persisted as she made her way to the Lake County Courthouse. The woman had learned her lesson about tardiness during the jury selection, so she arrived early. Other members of the panel dragged in one by one, but all arrived before the deadline. Once again, they waited past the appointed hour with no word from the bailiff. After a little over two hours past the time designated, the officer escorted the group into the court room.

"Seems a hair bit strange that nobody's here except the judge," the juror who had wanted to discuss the case previously whispered as he leaned toward Katy. "Wonder what's going on?"

"That is strange, "Katy replied. "No lawyers, no defendant, no one in the gallery."

When all jurors had taken their seats, the judge addressed them. "Ladies and gentlemen, there has been yet another delay. The court offers its sincere apologies. I know your lives have all been turned upside down, but your service is greatly appreciated. You may return to your homes to wait for further notification.

Remember my previous instructions: do not read news articles about the case, do not listen to radio or watch TV pieces about it, and do not, let me repeat, do not discuss the case with anyone. I mean no one, not even your spouse. The court is in recess until further notice."

* * *

"I was terribly upset," Katy exclaimed. "I wanted to get the unpleasant job over with. We all knew the prosecution would seek the death penalty, and you know my feelings on that. The delay just created more time for that to play on my mind."

"What on earth caused the additional delay?" Randy questioned.

"There was good cause, but it lasted longer than it should have. As the prosecution later proved, the scoundrel was guilty as sin, and there sure wasn't any good reason for the delay to drag on so long. Just a defense tactic."

* * *

"Gil, GIL! You'd best get back here real quick," deputy Long hollered from the area where barred cells secured prisoners.

"What's going on?" the sheriff asked as he rushed to the holding area. When he arrived at Herron's cell he observed the prisoner lying on his bunk covered in blood. "What the hell?"

"He done slit his wrist," Long responded.

"Get an ambulance here now! How in God's name did he get a hold of something to cut his wrist with?"

"It appears that at some point he kept a fork from his meal tray. There it is on the floor." Long informed. "Looks like he's had it for some time."

"Yeah. Appears like he used the concrete block wall as a grindstone to sharpen the thing," Gil noted as he spotted a scratched-up area of the wall partially hidden behind the bunk.

The emergency room doctor at the small Leadville hospital informed Gil that Herron had only cut himself superficially and no danger of death had resulted. *Too bad he didn't succeed,* the sheriff thought as he escorted Herron to the squad car for the return trip to jail. *That would a put an end to this nightmare and saved a lot of time and money. Shoulda shot the son-of-a-bitch dead before I called for backup that night. Cut it out, Gil. Don't be thinkin' like that. Let the system do its work.*

The attempted suicide aided the public defender's case since he intended an insanity defense. Lawyer Colton petitioned the judge for an evaluation by a credible psychiatrist who interviewed the alleged rapist and murderer numerous times.

"Your honor, after extensive sessions with Mr. Herron, it is my professional opinion that he is not competent to stand trial at this time. He in no way would be able to aid in his own defense. It is my recommendation that he be placed in an institution for further evaluation and therapy," the doctor testified.

"It is the decision of this court that the defendant, Richard Herron Jr be remanded to the Colorado asylum for the criminally insane in Pueblo County," the judge ruled. "He is to remain there until such time that he is declared competent to stand trial."

Most folks figured that the ever-cunning Herron never intended suicide, but only used the tactic as a delay.

* * *

"Once again, I became more or less a prisoner in my own home," Katy declared. "Oh, I could go about business in Leadville, you know, taking kids to school or the sitter, shopping, and going to work, but I couldn't leave town. Had to stay close and wait for the notice that the trial would reconvene. They told us if we weren't home to get the call they'd send the sheriff looking for us."

"Well, that sucked," Randy asserted.

"I guess so," Katy replied. "Whatever that means. One of the worst parts of the whole situation was working where I had to face the public. Everybody in town knew I was on the jury and a lot of 'em wanted to talk about it. The boss had warned the other workers to keep their mouths shut and not be bothering me about it, but it was hard to keep the customers quiet. Basically, I just ignored the talk and the questions. Couldn't do much of anything else."

* * *

Katy quickly removed herself from the dining room at the High Country Café when a customer who had probably had one too many Coors hollered, "Hey, Katy, you gonna burn that son of a bitch?"

The questions and harassment persisted and escalated to the point that the owner of the establishment posted a large sign at the entrance. *THE HIGH COUNTRY CAFÉ IS A HERRON FREE ZONE. NO TALK OF THE DEFENDANT OR THE CASE IS ALLOWED. IF THIS IS NOT ACCEPTABLE GO TO THE GOLDEN BURRO CAFÉ.* Most patrons got the message and willingly complied with the declaration since they thought highly of their favorite waitress and the High Country served the best food in Leadville. Regular customers knew Katy's limitations about discussion of the case and they respected that, but some of the rougher element of the town purposely dined at the cafe just for the opportunity to stir things up. Many times, the owner escorted those out who did not abide by the "Herron free zone." Business at the establishment had been built on tourists and regulars, thus the loss of the infrequent troublemaker diners had little or no effect on profits.

Time dragged by for Katy although she felt gratitude that the delay allowed her time with the kids during their summer vacation from school. She feared that stress of the situation had taken its toll on her and reflected in her attitude with the children. As a defense against what she considered an unacceptable stance, the caring mother spent every hour away from work with Brandon, Hunter, and baby Brenda. Normally on her days off, prior to her selection to the jury, Katy took her family to historical places like Fairplay, Blackhawk, Cripple Creek, or the numerous museums in Denver, but they spent the summer of 1981 close to home.

Even though Katy had enjoyed the summer spent with her children, she had hoped for a conclusion of the trial before cold fall and winter weather set in. Most years Old Man Winter commenced his assault on the high-mountain town in mid- to late September and he made no exception in 1981. Cold north winds chilled Katy to the bone as she parked her car and carried groceries she purchased at Safeway into the house. As she unlocked and opened the front door she heard the phone ringing persistently.

"Mrs. Edmond? This is the sheriff's office," the voice on the phone informed.

"Yes, this is Katy Edmond. What can I do for you?"

"I'm calling to notify you that you must report to the courthouse tomorrow at 9:00 am. The defendant has been returned from Pueblo and the trial is scheduled to begin."

The jury heard no mention of Herron's mental health before they took their seats in the jury box except that the psychiatrists at the Colorado Asylum for the criminally insane had declared the defendant competent to stand trial. Katy dreaded the proceedings, but at least the long wait had ended, and the process had begun.

"Not guilty by reason of insanity," lawyer Colton declared when the judge asked how the defendant would plead.

The trial proceeded as the prosecution delivered their opening arguments. They insisted evidence would prove Herron's guilt beyond any reasonable doubt and that they were seeking the death penalty. "The only reasonable verdict is 'guilty,'" the lead prosecutor declared before he finally sat down after he had spoken for a considerable amount of time.

The defense lawyer offered his opening statement as he declared the defendant's insanity. He asserted that Herron did not know right from wrong when he committed the offense and aid in his own defense had been rendered impossible by his mental state and demanded the jury find him not-guilty. Colton raved on for nearly an hour before he concluded, "the only reasonable verdict is 'not guilty.'"

Guilty. Not guilty. Reasonable verdict. Can't aid in his own defense. Beyond any reasonable doubt. The declarations of the day ran amuck in Katy's mind as she unsuccessfully sought sleep. *Looks like they're gonna drag this out forever. Sure hope they prove guilt or not guilty without question,* she thought. The nightmares had begun, and they continued throughout the trial and beyond.

Gil Gentry testified for several days as to what he found at the crime scene near Turquois Lake. He told of the glove of skin, the tennis shoes and gas can they found in the wash, Herron's jockey shorts located at the top of the rise where the rape had taken place, pieces of burnt flesh found along a blood trail, and many other gruesome details. As the sheriff related the horrific events, an unknown force drew his eyes toward the attractive woman who sat in the front row of the jury box. Numerous times their eyes met and the distress that he noted on her face melted the big, tough, masculine sheriff's heart. He had great empathy for all the jurors as they held the life of the defendant in their hands, but with Katy he felt a difference. He remembered when he had informed her of the death of her husband and that her world had crumbled. At that time, her obvious pregnancy added to the stress and in December of that year added the responsibility of a third child to the young widow. *It just ain't right. Why would they put her on this jury? It just ain't right,* he thought as his testimony continued.

* * *

"All the testimony was gruesome and heart-rending," Katy avowed. "But the crime scene photos were the worst part, I think."

"I'm so sorry you had to go through all that, darlin'," Gil comforted. "It just wasn't right puttin' you on that jury. What with three kids to care for and bein' a widow. Just wasn't right."

"I guess they did what they had to do," Katy replied. "The prosecution and the defense disqualified so many jurors mainly for their stance of capital punishment. The prosecutor didn't want anybody that was totally against the death penalty and the defense lawyer sure didn't want anybody that was for it. That eliminated a lot of folks and I think my statement about the subject sealed my fate. I told the truth. I could assess the death penalty if guilt was proven beyond any doubt and I think Colton was arrogant enough that he thought he could plant doubt with his insanity plea. As far as him claiming that Herron didn't know right from wrong, that is total BS. Even the most deranged know it's not right to rape, torture, and murder."

"Some folks might tend to argue with you on that point, but I agree with you," Randy asserted.

"The nightmare got considerable worse when the medical examiner testified."

* * *

"It was obvious that Herron knew that Marcia was still alive when he doused her with gas and set her on fire," the medical examiner testified.

"How so?" the prosecutor asked.

"She had to have been in a standing position when he poured the gas on her," he answered.

Folks in the gallery gasped and many people covered their eyes as the medical examiner displayed a gruesome, blown-up copy of a picture of the victim's body.

"As you can see in these photos, the accelerant ran from her upper body and torso down her legs. Left streaks on her legs. There's no way it could have done that unless she was upright. Oh, she was alive, all right, and the sick bastard knew it."

"Objection," Colton shouted. "Prejudicial."

"Objection sustained," the judge declared. "The jury will disregard that last statement."

Testimony continued for several weeks with many heated exchanges between prosecution and defense. Objections abounded, the judge sustained some, and overruled others. The two fishermen, George and Barry, Deputy Long, and numerous other witnesses portrayed the assault, rape, and murder of Marcia Leggett so vividly and with such conviction that apparently, no doubt entered the minds of most the twelve men and women charged with the determination of guilt or innocence.

The trial concluded with final arguments by the prosecution first, followed by the defense. Herron squirmed and shifted in his chair with an arrogant smirk on his face as the lead prosecutor recounted all the horrifying events and cited all the explicit gory detail.

"In view of all the evidence the only possible verdict is guilty," he concluded.

As lawyer Colton began his final arguments, Herron jumped up from his seat and ranted, "I killed the bitch. She wouldn't give me what I wanted so I took it anyway then I killed the slut. Nobody turns Richard Herron down, nobody. She got what was coming to her."

"Sit down and shut up," Lawyer Colton demanded as he grabbed Herron's arm and pulled him down into his chair.

"You shoulda seen her when she went up in flames. It was a beautiful sight to behold," the defendant shouted as he pulled away from the attorney and stood up.

Several sheriff's deputies restrained Herron before he made further statements. The trial had ended, the judge sent the jury out for deliberations, with an admonition that the ravings of the defendant be disregarded.

* * *

"You can't un-ring a bell," Katy declared. "As far as I was concerned, the rantings of Herron were no less than a confession. He was guilty. Apparently, it also made up the minds of most of the other eleven.

"What do you mean most of the others?" Randy questioned.

"Believe it or not, one guy was a holdout."

* * *

"Herron is obviously guilty as charged," the jury foreman announced. "Let's just have a quick vote and get this over with."

"Hold on just a minute," the dissenting juror demanded. "He was definitely insane. Nobody does stuff like that unless they are insane."

"Come, on. Give us a break," the foreman responded. "The doctor from the asylum declared him competent."

"I don't care. Kinda feel sorry for the guy, being rejected by the victim like that."

"Good grief! Are you a total idiot? That don't make it okay. He has to pay for what he did," another juror asserted.

"Aren't you the guy that wanted to 'burn' him even before the trial started, and now you feel sorry for the murdering rapist?" Katy questioned vehemently. "What kind a nut case are you anyway? Maybe I'll tell the judge that you talked about the case inappropriately and just maybe he'll send you to jail for contempt."

Tensions in the deliberation room accelerated as all eyes turned toward another juror when he spoke. "Hell, Herron's old man just had to keep the rugrats and his old lady in line. A backhand now and again don't hurt nobody. His father didn't do no more to him than me and most guys do to discipline our kids and keep our old ladies on their toes, and we ain't all insane. It's just a copout."

Katy and the others sat in stunned silence as they reflected on the outburst.

* * *

"That guy should not have been on that jury," Gil declared. "He sure as hell was not an objective observer. He was kinda new in town. He'd barely been here long enough to qualify as a potential juror and nobody really knew anything much about him, but after the trial I was called out to his house on domestic violence complaints several times. He really belonged in jail, but the wife would not file charges."

"Well, he for sure had it all wrong when he said most guys acted that way," Randy asserted. "I cannot believe the guy that wanted to burn Herron originally was the lone holdout."

"I never understood what he was thinking, but the threat of jail changed his mind," Katy informed. "He knew I was serious and he remembered how adamant the judge had been, so he yielded. We took one vote and found Herron guilty as charged. Only took a few minutes."

"Didn't the judge think it was kind a strange that it only took a few minutes?" Randy questioned.

"The foreman didn't call for the bailiff right away. We all just sat there in stunned silence for a couple of hours and finally he informed the bailiff that we had reached a decision."

"Well, at least it was over," Randy declared.

"Not quite," Katy responded. "The punishment phase of the trial didn't begin until two weeks later."

* * *

Katy slept little in the interim as all the horrifying events, the rape, the murder, and the burning body swirled about in her troubled mind. *Gas running down her legs. Oh, God, he knew she was alive and set her on fire anyway. What made him think he had the right to take what he wanted. Chunks of flesh and burnt skin strewn along a trail of blood.* The nightmare continued until the punishment phase and beyond. Katy experienced the rape and murder night after night for months. Over the ensuing years the gruesome events occasionally invaded her dreams until Herron got the needle.

CHAPTER 17

THE PUNISHMENT

THE JURORS ENCOUNTERED ANOTHER AGONIZING WAIT AS THE two-week interim dragged by. The options they faced provoked serious considerations for Katy since she did not like the idea of the death penalty, but she hated what Herron had done even more. The criminal obviously had no redeeming value, he had shown no sign of remorse, but instead he had declared that the victim got what she deserved. Civilized society had no place for the murdering rapist. No doubt as to his guilt existed, but even so Katy detested making a decision normally left to God. The vexing thoughts constantly consumed her troubled mind and she yearned for the long-awaited conclusion of the case.

Sure hope this doesn't take too long, Katy thought as she drove toward the county courthouse. *I've never liked the idea of the death penalty, but what Herron did has changed my mind. There is no doubt that he is guilty, and after what he did to that poor girl he deserves to lose his life. An eye for an eye.* She kind of figured that the jurors all felt the same way and a swift assessment of punishment seemed highly likely.

The screeching sounds of horns and sirens pierced her ears and filled the air as Katy neared the courthouse. She feared that the blocked traffic insured her tardiness and she knew how the judge felt about that. A huge crowd filled the courthouse parking lot and a vast contingent of humanity blocked a large portion of Harrison Avenue. Katy took the first available parking place a block or so away and hurriedly walked the additional distance. When she arrived at the courthouse parking lot, she observed signs that members of the crowd carried. STOP THE KILLING, TWO WRONGS DON'T MAKE A RIGHT, JUDGMENT BELONGS TO GOD. HERRON IS A VICTIM. Folks on the opposite side of the street shouted, "All you bleeding hearts need to go back to Denver where you came from." "What happens in Leadville ain't none of your business." "If it had been your daughter you'd be hollering to burn 'im."

* * *

"Herron is a victim?" Randy asked. "What kind of nut thought that?"

"Oh, some of those bleedin' hearts kinda zeroed in on the abuse heaped on him by his father," Gil answered.

"He did suffer an ungodly upbringing," Katy noted. "But that's no excuse for what he did."

* * *

The shouts of the two opposing views got louder and uglier until a scuffle erupted between the two factions and an all-out battle ensued as many people from both sides jumped into the fracas. Screams and shouts reverberated through the throng of protesters as blood squirted from broken noses and busted lips. Although totally outnumbered, Gil and his deputies forced their way in between the two groups, but calm did not return.

Out of sheer desperation and against his better judgement, the sheriff pulled his revolver, fired two shots in the air, and the crowd became silent. Gil put a fog horn to his lips and shouted. "I will not tolerate this kind of behavior in Leadville. You people from Denver have the right to protest, but it's got to be peaceable. Any further physical altercations and you will all be arrested. You folks from Leadville don't let these bleeding hearts pull you into a fight."

The two groups separated, but the opponents of the death penalty lined the courthouse parking lot and gathered near the door. The folks from Leadville respected the sheriff, most dispersed, and the few that remained gathered on the opposite side of Harrison Avenue. One of Gil's deputies had assembled the jurors at a safe distance from the fracas. Tension filled the atmosphere as they approached the building. The rowdy activists shouted demands for a lighter sentence at those who held Herron's fate in their hands.

"Who do you sanctimonious hypocrites think you are? Give the man a few years behind bars where he can think about what he's done and come away cured of his sickness."

"Don't be self-righteous. Judgment belongs to the Almighty."

"Send him back to Pueblo."

"Give him death and we will bring down the fires of hell on you."

Some of the comments got downright nasty and threatening. Gil and his deputies escorted the jurors through the crowd and stayed close until they arrived safely in the jury room.

* * *

"I'd never seen or heard anything like it," Katy exclaimed. "Scared the bejeebers out of me."

"I bet it did," Randy responded. "I've heard of such things, but I've never witnessed them and I sure as heck was never in the kind of position you were in."

"By the time we got to the jury room, I was shaking all over."

"Darlin', I'm so sorry you had to go through all that," Gil comforted. "You shoulda never been on that jury. I just don't know what that judge was thinkin'."

* * *

The first day of the punishment phase dragged by for Katy and the other jurors as the prosecutor and the defense lawyer presented arguments for and against the death penalty. The seemingly useless discourse that dominated the proceedings appeared of little value since apparently the jurors each had their own opinion about the punishment. As the day finally came to an end, the group again faced the protestors outside. Out of fear of arrest, the raucous throng had quieted down considerably, the group said little, but they shot hateful glares at the departing jurors.

As Katy turned off Harrison Avenue she observed a sheriff's department car that was apparently following her. When she stopped at the babysitter's and collected Brenda she noted the same vehicle parked down the street. *Wonder why they're following me,* Katy thought as she drove toward home with the squad car close behind. When the confused woman pulled into her driveway and the pursuer parked a short distance away, she noted that Sheriff Gil Gentry sat behind the wheel.

Many years ago, I mighta been right out there with that group, protesting and carrying a sign, but they didn't have to suffer through this ungodly trial and see firsthand what that madman did. Real life changes your perspective, Katy thought as she again experienced a sleepless night. *After the horrible things he did to Marcia, no punishment is bad enough. The law won't let us give him what he really deserves, but I reckon he'll burn in hell and we can dispatch him there real quick.* She had no realization of how long the appeals process in capital punishment cases took and that many times delayed justice only came decades later.

When the morning sun finally peeked through the mountains in the east, Katy dragged herself from bed, showered, dressed, and prepared breakfast for her three children. While she bundled them up as a defense against the bitter cold Colorado weather, she glanced out her front window and observed the sheriff's car still parked down the street. "You kids stay inside, I'll be back directly," she instructed as she pulled on her coat, walked out the door, and marched in a deliberate manner toward the squad car still occupied by Gil Gentry. The scrutiny that Katy apparently faced infuriated her, and she wanted an explanation as to why the sheriff followed her and kept her house under surveillance. As the highly annoyed woman approached, the sheriff pulled out from the curb and drove away, but he did not go far. When she headed out with the kids in the car, once again he followed, waited down the street when she stopped at the babysitter's, and continued the pursuit as she drove toward the courthouse.

When the concerned woman arrived at her destination she observed the same groups as the day before. The protestors against the death penalty still carried the signs and marched back and forth in front of the building. The good citizens of Leadville remained on the opposite side of Harrison Avenue, ready for a fight. Many of Gil's deputies had assembled and they escorted Katy and the other jurors inside.

The panel of adjudicators grew extremely tired of the same seemingly unnecessary process as the day before continued for nearly a week. At the end of each day's proceedings, Gil followed Katy until she arrived safely at home and every morning he tailed her until she reached the jury room. Several times the disgruntled woman approached the car occupied by Sheriff Gentry, but he drove away before she reached his location.

* * *

"Why wouldn't you talk to Katy?" Randy questioned.

"It just wouldn't 'a looked right," Gil answered. "Everybody knew how I felt about Herron. I wanted to see 'em stick the needle to 'im. If somebody, especially some of the outsiders from Denver had seen us talkin', they'd 'a made something of it, her bein' a juror and all. Probably woulda claimed I was tryin' to influence her in some way and I didn't want to do anything to upset the apple cart. Like everybody else, I just wanted the whole thing over and done with."

"Why were you following her?"

"He had good reason," Katy chimed in appreciatively.

* * *

Unbeknownst to Katy, during the rowdy confrontations between the protestors and the people of Leadville, Gil and his deputies heard numerous threats hurled against the jurors. It seemed as a paradox to the sheriff when he heard death threats against the members of the panel from the faction that protested capital punishment. In the event of a death penalty decision, they planned retribution against the decision makers, their families, friends, and homes. There had even been talk of "an eye for an eye" if the jury assessed the ultimate punishment.

With assistance from the small Leadville Police Department, Gil assigned a deputy or a city cop as protection for each member of the panel. He became Katy's protector as well as an admirer. From that day when their eyes met during the trial the bachelor sheriff had developed an attraction for the young attractive widow. Katy also had similar thoughts of her own, but since she did not know the reason for the surveillance she felt harassed. She had no idea that officers kept a close eye on the other jurors. The same scenario continued throughout the punishment phase of the trial.

On the eighth day of the proceedings, emotions in the courtroom heated up. Many people in the chamber shed tears and tension filled the space as family members and friends of Marcia Leggett spoke directly to the murdering rapist, Richard Herron.

Marcia's friend, Linda, sobbed loudly and wiped the flow of moisture from her face as she spoke. "You robbed me of my best friend," she cried. "I'll never see her again. Not only did you take her away, but you tortured her something fierce after you done raped her before you killed her. Ain't nothing human about you. You ain't nothing but a filthy animal. Hope the devil pours gas on you before he throws you in the lake of fire."

Herron sat with a devilish smirk on his face as he listened to the heart-rending declaration. As Linda spoke, Herron became excited and aroused as it renewed his lecherous fantasies. His demeanor and attitude experienced no change, rather the emotional declarations by Linda served as a turn-on to the pervert. *Some way, some how, some day I'm gonna have a go at that girl,* he thought. By confronting Herron directly, Linda felt part of the burden that plagued her soul had been relieved however, she never forgot the horrific way that he had taken her friend away.

Several of Marcia's brothers expressed similar feelings toward the defendant, but the experience helped little with their grief. Esther Leggett remained stoic and devoid of detectable emotions as she spoke briefly. The woman still laid much of the blame for her daughter's murder at the feet of her husband.

The victim's father spoke in hushed tones in between sobs. "You done took away the most precious thing in my life, my only daughter. I will never hear her laugh again. I'll not have her to comfort when she cries for she will no longer be there to share her sorrows. There'll be no more goodnight kisses, no more silly, girly talk, and no high school graduation. I'll not be able to walk her down the aisle and place her hand in the hand of her intended.

She won't be there to give me grandkids." He pulled a handkerchief from his pocket and wiped away the tears that flowed like the Arkansas River flows down the mountains. "You have broke my heart. Wish you had killed me. Oh, God, I cannot bear it." The grieving father collapsed to the floor and as a couple of Gil's men helped him up the murdering rapist shouted.

"She got what she deserved. Nobody turns Richard Herron down. She sure was fine and she made a spectacular sight when she went up in flames."

Howard pulled away from the deputies and lunged at Herron who broke out in devilish laughter. Before the officers restrained him, the father grabbed the fiend around the waist, threw him to the floor, sat astraddle on the villain, and beat him in the face repeatedly. *Wham, wham,* the judge pounded the gavel on the bench. "Officers, get Mr. Leggett out of here. Mr. Leggett, I fully understand your feelings, but I cannot allow such an outburst in my courtroom."

The lawmen escorted Howard from the chamber, but no charges against him ever occurred. The judge had complete empathy for the man since he had a daughter about the same age as Marcia. A rumor circulated that the magistrate had privately hoped for the death penalty and that he had related how he would like to have executed Herron himself.

As calm returned to the courtroom, the judge spoke directly to the jury. "You must disregard that outburst. I charge you to think about every consideration that has been presented to this court and make an unbiased determination as to the punishment that the defendant will receive. The prosecution has asked for the death penalty and you may assess death, but you may also give him life in prison. The decision is yours. Bailiff, please escort the jury to the jury room."

* * *

"Deciding his punishment took a little longer than the guilty verdict," Katy informed.

"I figured it went real fast," Randy replied. "The crimes were horrific, and he was guilty as sin. He admitted in open court that he did it."

"Yes, but deciding to put another human being to death weighed heavy on most of the jurors."

"I don't think he was human," Randy asserted. "You'd shoot a rabid dog and he was a lot worse than that."

"That's pretty much how I felt about it," Katy responded. "But, several of the others had different ideas."

* * *

"Let's have a quick vote and get this over with," the jury foreman suggested.

"Wait just minute," one of the jurors protested. "We need to think about this before we condemn a man to death. That's a decision that's normally made by the Almighty."

"You think the Almighty decided for that madman to rape and murder Marcia?" Katy questioned passionately.

"Well, . . .ah . . . no. . . . but."

"Let's take a vote," the foreman insisted. "All in favor of giving him death hold up your hands." Eleven jurors raised their hands, but the dissenter did not.

"You want that animal running loose?" another juror questioned.

"He ain't gonna be running loose. He'll be behind bars for life."

"You ever hear of parole?" the foreman questioned. "This is not a federal case and there's always the possibility of parole, later on."

"I could not live with myself if we gave him life and he got out on parole," Katy asserted.

"You know the state of Colorado is leaning liberal," the foreman suggested. "We get one of those bleeding hearts for a governor years from now, and he's liable to pardon the S.O.B. Is that what you want?"

The argument continued for several hours and it seemed that the mind of the lone holdout could not be changed.

"You got any kids?" Katy asked the hold out.

"Yep, got myself one sweet beautiful little girl."

"How old is your daughter?" Katy questioned.

"Just turned four."

"Picture this: your sweet beautiful four-year-old little girl grows into a real good-looking teenager, a madman like Herron abducts her, takes her out to the lake, beats the crap out of her, rips her clothes off, throws his own britches and shorts aside, and violates your sweet beautiful daughter over and over before he douses her with gas and sets her on fire when she tries to get away. Picture that and then tell me he deserves to live," Katy pleaded passionately. "If you think he deserves to live, you're as sick a scumbag as him."

The other ten jurors stood simultaneously and applauded for an extended time before the lone holdout spoke sheepishly. "Well, ah, since you, ah, put it like that. Well. . ."

"Well, what?" the foreman questioned. "You ready to change your vote or do you want the monster to come back and do your 'sweet beautiful baby' in? What's it gonna be? Let's take another vote. All in favor of giving the bastard death raise your hand."

* * *

"That time the vote was unanimous," Katy informed.

"Darlin', I was real proud that you spoke up and convinced that idiot. Still am," Gil declared as he placed his arm around Katy and planted a big kiss on her.

"Me too, Katy," Randy chimed in. "The idea that scumbag might have gone free at some point is just unbelievable."

"Well, ain't gonna happen," Gil added. "I saw 'im dispatched to hell."

* * *

Glad that the proceedings had ended, Katy gave out a sigh of relief as she drove down Harrison Avenue headed for home. She looked in the rearview mirror where she spotted the sheriff who followed her again. *This is gonna stop right here and now,* the agitated woman thought as she slammed on the brakes, threw her car in park, emerged from the vehicle and marched toward the sheriff's car. She had stopped so suddenly that Gil's squad car skidded within inches of Katy's bumper. This time he did not get away.

"Why do you keep following me like I'm some kind of criminal?" she shouted.

"Just settle yourself down, Mrs. Edmond. I've got good reason."

The broad-shouldered masculine man spoke gently as he explained the danger perpetrated by the group from Denver. The angered look on her face melted away into an appreciative smile as she thought, *How could I have thought he had anything but good intentions? He's so soft-spoken, kind, and caring and good-looking too. I think I could fall for this man.*

Gil had thoughts of his own. *Oh geez, I think I'm in love. I want to protect that sweet woman for the rest of her life.*

* * *

"It was love and we both knew it," Katy asserted as she looked at Gil adoringly. "He was my hero and I wanted to spend the rest of my life with the best man around."

"I knew right then and there that I had found my one and only," Gil responded. "I sure as hell ain't the best, but darlin', you sure are. You changed my life and I'll always love you for that."

"Ah, ain't that sweet," Randy chuckled. "You two don't get all mushy on me now."

"Well, as they say, 'the rest is history," Gil avowed as he returned the look of adoration.

"Just one question," Randy noted. "What about that wild group from Denver? Did they cause any more problems?"

"Heck no," Gil answered. "They was all talk and no action, thankfully. They tucked their tails and headed back to Denver."

* * *

Richard Herron's dark pensive eyes remained wide open with an evil stare, but his body went limp. The prison doctor pronounced the inmate dead at 12:01 AM, on Thursday, April 22, 2009, three decades after the time he committed unthinkable crimes. Even though the wheels of the Colorado judicial system had turned slowly, Gil Gentry knew that justice for Marcia Leggett had at long last been served. The retired sheriff of Lake County took no real pleasure in the execution, because the victim still lay dead in the Evergreen Cemetery on the northwestern edge of Leadville, and thirty years later her family still mourned.

CHAPTER 18

THE EPILOGUE

EVEN THOUGH THEY NEVER FORGOT THE HORRIFIC RAPE AND murder of Marcia Leggett, life returned to normal in Leadville, Colorado. Tourists and fishermen swelled the population in the summer and ski enthusiasts visited from surrounding areas in winter. The townspeople went about their daily business, but the thought of the maniac rarely deserted their psyche. The crazed madman, Richard Herron, went to death row in the prison at Canon City and ultimately received the needle.

The sheriff's and the juror's courtroom attraction resulted in a whirlwind courtship and they married a few months later. Gil's "itchy" feet and wandering ways faded away and he became the epitome of stability. Katy's three children had a new father who treated them as his own and he exerted great positive influence over their lives. The three grew into model and productive citizens. Lake County had a permanent well-respected sheriff for many years. The lawman became legendary in his pursuit and capture of many criminals, but none so vile as Richard Herron.

After Gil retired from the Lake County Sheriff's Department he continued his unrelenting pursuit of bad guys in a capacity as a private investigator. The retired lawman had become legendary throughout the country in his quest for law and justice.

Each time Randy and Barbara visited with his favorite uncle, the man told many tales of crimes he had solved and scumbags he had arrested in his pursuit of justice. Randy would later write a novel based on his uncle's involvement in the Richard Herron case, and with each of the exciting tales of law and order that Gil related, he made notes, and considered the idea of more novels in the future.

Esther Leggett blamed her husband for the death of their child, but they stayed together in a frosty relationship until death parted them. Herron not only ended Marcia's life, but he also caused dissention and near ruin of the Leggett family. The deep grief that Howard felt plagued him for the remainder of his life, but he carried on as best he could for the sake of his chilly wife and his other children. It has been reported that as the sad old man lay on his death bed he reached out and called Marcia's name just before he departed his earthly life. "Marcia, Marcia baby, is that you? Have you come for me?"

"Yes, Daddy, it's me. Take my hand and I'll lead you on your journey."

Howard closed his eyes and a look of serenity that folks had not seen in many years came across his face. After all the years of agony and torment the tortured soul finally received peace.

After the execution, numerous campers have sworn that they have seen Richard Herron stalking the mountain near Turquoise Lake where he brutally raped and murdered Marcia Leggett. The site became known as "Terror Mountain," a name appropriate for the area where the horrific crime took place. Many times, flames have been spotted near the place where the mad man set his victim on fire when she tried to escape, but upon investigation no fires have been found. They say he wanders with a crazed expression as he looks for something. Some believe he's not satisfied with what he did to Marcia, and he's looking for her so that he can brutalize her again.

A few times early on folks reported that they heard screams that emanated from the gulley where the rapist set the girl on fire. They claimed to have seen Marcia as she roamed the area half naked with a look of terror on her face, but those sightings discontinued after Gil delivered Herron to death row.

Are these stories figments of wild imaginations or are they factual sightings? Who knows? Many residents in the area will tell you they are real without a doubt, but others will swear it's all made up. The next time you're in Colorado, make a sojourn to Leadville, have a burger at the Golden Burro Café or chicken fried steak at the High County Café before you take the road west out of town, past the Honey Loaf Campground, and up the mountain to the lake. Forget about the Silver King Inn and spend the night on "Terror Mountain" if you dare, and decide for yourself.

About the Author

Fred L. Funk was born and raised in North Texas near Denton. He attended what is now the University of North Texas, but transferred to East Texas State College to pursue a pre-theology degree. While attending ETSC, he pastored several Methodist churches in North and East Texas as a supply pastor. He later switched careers to accounting and finance, and worked for a national retail furniture chain for thirty-five years.

Now retired, Fred is an active member and former president of the Denton Noon Kiwanis Club and a Past Lieutenant Governor of the Texas-Oklahoma District of Kiwanis International. When he filled in at the last minute one day for a speaker who didn't show up, he told some tales from his preaching days. The response was very favorable, and members of the club encouraged him by saying, "You ought to write a book!" So he did. Then he wrote another, and another. And he is working on yet another. Once he got started, he just can't stop.

He and his wife, Dana, have been married more than fifty years. They have two daughters and a son, seven grandchildren, and three great-grandchildren.